Author of the "street lit insta-classic" *(The Washington Post)*
Let That Be the Reason,

VICKIE M. STRINGER

is "the queen of gangsta lit" *(Metro Times,* Detroit).

Praise for her *Essence* bestselling series featuring the unforgettable hustlers Bacon, Q and Red

DIRTIER THAN EVER

"Urban street lit doesn't get any dirtier than Stringer's series. . . . Well-paced action and Red's relentless anger keep the pages turning. . . . A cliffhanger ending indicates we haven't seen the last of raunchy Red."

—*Publishers Weekly*

DIRTY RED

"A calculatedly nasty yet redemptive tale of a ruthless woman. . . . [A] savvy street thriller."

—*Booklist*

"The 'queen   cast of char-acters in this   ampa Tribune

These titles are also available as ebooks.

Dirtier Than Ever

A NOVEL

VICKIE M. STRINGER

ATRIA PAPERBACK

New York London Toronto Sydney

ATRIA PAPERBACK

A Division of Simon & Schuster, Inc.
1230 Avenue of the Americas
New York, NY 10020

First Atria Paperback hardcover edition February 2011

ATRIA PAPERBACK and colophon are trademarks of
Simon & Schuster, Inc.

For information about special discounts for bulk purchases,
please contact Simon & Schuster Special Sales at
1-866-506-1949 or business@simonandschuster.com.

The Simon & Schuster Speakers Bureau can bring authors to your
live event. For more information or to book an event, contact the
Simon & Schuster Speakers Bureau at 1-866-248-3049 or visit our
website at www.simonspeakers.com.

Manufactured in the United States of America

10 9 8 7 6 5 4 3 2 1

Th Library of Congress has cataloged the hardcover edition as follows:
Stringer, Vickie M.
    Dirtier than ever : a novel / Vickie M. Stringer. — 1st Atria Books
hardcover ed.
        p.   cm.
    1. African American women—Fiction.   I. Title.
    PS3569.T69586D56   2010
    813'.54—dc22   2009049423

ISBN 978-1-4391-6611-6
ISBN 978-1-4391-6612-3 (pbk)
ISBN 978-1-4391-6613-0 (ebook)

Michael L. Haggen
This one's for you!

Warning comes before destruction.

—Pastor Eric F. Mitchell

Dirtier Than Ever

Q drove away from the bank, not knowing what to do. He hated the ground Red walked on and wished that Bacon would have killed her when he had the chance. Red had played him the entire time. She had known that the check she presented to him was no good. It was $1.6 million worth of lies. She knew that he had stopped hustling, and she knew that he was counting on this money to tide them over and to get things going on the business tip. She had promised him that the money didn't mean a thing, and that she would give it all up to be with him. And he had fallen for it hook, line and sinker. He had listened to her bullshit, but now he realized that her word was as worthless as the voided check he held in his hand. "You scandalous, triflin' bitch," Q bit out through his gritted teeth.

A single beep rang from his cell phone. Q looked at it; one missed call from Detective Thomas.

"What the fuck he want?" Q asked, irritated.

Thomas had been calling him for the past couple of days, but

Q had never returned his calls. He was tired of Thomas's badgering and accusations. He was tired of going over the same shit with him on different days. Q was tired of him, period.

Q drove to the closest liquor store. He needed something strong enough to wash out the disgusting taste Red left in his mouth. Afterward he hightailed it back to the loft. He wanted to be there when Red came home for the evening so he could kick her ass out of his house and his life, permanently.

Once inside the loft, Q plopped down on the couch. He was mentally exhausted. Shaking his head in disgust, he looked around at the décor and thought about Red. He began drinking at the mere thought of her.

An hour later, Q was feeling real good and on chill mode. Just as he laid his head back and the heaviness of his eyelids began to take over, he was startled by a loud noise.

"Wha . . . whadefuckisdat?" he slurred heavily. His head drooped forward and he saw a now-empty bottle of Martel. "Stoppit," he slurred again, looking at the bottle until he realized it was the phone ringing. He reached over to the end table with a heavy hand to pick up the cordless phone.

"Yella," he answered.

"Mr. Carter?"

"Who wans ta know?" Q's tongue felt four inches thick and his face felt numb.

"This is Detective Thomas. I need to see you about Ezekiel's murder. I just got a hold of the toxicology report and there's something I think you'd be interested in knowing."

"Yeah . . . yeah . . ." Q sighed. The detective had been calling him nonstop, bugging him about Zeke's death since it happened. The questioning soon turned into something Q wasn't comfortable with. It was as if the detective were trying to accuse him of having something to do with Zeke's death—or, at the very least, knowing who did.

"I also think you need to know we found a vid—"

"You know what you need to know?" Q spoke boldly into the phone.

"What, Mr. Carter? Do you have something that can help with the case?" Detective Thomas said eagerly.

"You need to know that you are an annoying-ass nigga. You and all your wannabe cop cronies. You can kiss my ass and do your own fucking work." Q pressed the "off" button.

Bacon yanked Red's head back until it couldn't go any farther. He wanted to snap her neck so bad that his dick started to get hard. He had finally gotten his hands on her and it felt good. Knowing that money was a big motivator for Red, Bacon had browsed the local real estate listings under Gomez Realty, disguising his voice and then posing as a prospective client with an offer he knew she couldn't refuse. After he mentioned that he had a sizable down payment for the property he liked, Red had suggested the property on Colonnade and made an appointment to meet him there. Just like he knew she would, Red took the bait—but he couldn't believe that she actually had the nerve to come back to *his* crib, the crib she had previously tried to sell, the same crib she had been fucking other niggas up in, the very same crib she now was trying to sell him. Bacon glared over at the king-size bed and grew even angrier. He could imagine Red being in his master bedroom, in his bed, with other men, while he had been on lockdown struggling to survive. She was supposed to be wifey, supposed to have held him down, but she didn't, and now she would answer for everything that she had done.

"Bacon, please," Red cried quietly. A tear rolled down her cheek.

Bacon stared coldly at her, let out an evil cackle and stood. *Smack!* He backhanded her.

"Bacon!" Red cried out and clasped her cheek.

Smack! He backhanded her again.

Red shot him a poisoned look. Not only had he slapped her once but the bastard had hit her twice. She rose to her feet.

"Bitch, I ain't say you can get up!" Bacon slapped her again, causing her to stumble. "You move when I say you can move!"

She got back on the floor.

"You dirty bitch!" Bacon shouted and raised his hand to her again.

Red was cold with fear. She hadn't seen this side of Bacon in quite a while.

"Now crawl!" he commanded.

With the back of her hand, Red wiped away the tears that were streaming down like a river. "B-Bacon, you been watching too much TV." She recalled how he liked this particular scene in the movie *Sparkle*, but she couldn't play it out for him.

"That's all I had time to do when I was locked down while you was spending all my shit! So bitch, I said crawl." Bacon pointed his .357 Magnum at her. "Or die."

Red knew she should have taken his guns out of the safe when she first thought about it, but now it was too late.

With the gun still pointed at her, Bacon reached and pulled a blue bag off the bed and opened it. Red stayed in the position she was in. Bacon reached into the bag, grabbed a stack of money and threw it down near his feet. Red eyeballed the money. Bacon reached again and threw another stack down next to the first one. Red recognized the band colors that held the money, and calculated that he had just dropped 50 g's right in front of her.

"You know you want this," Bacon taunted her. "Now you know what it's like to be broke, huh? Crawl!"

Red began crawling.

Bacon reached into the bag and dropped more stacks of money on the floor.

Red crawled more. *Your available balance is $1. Now you know what's it's like to be broke, huh?* echoed repeatedly in her head. Everything she had been through was for nothing. She was back at square one, back to having nothing. Nada. She struggled her entire life to make a way for herself in a world that had been stacked against her, and now her entire life's struggle had been reduced to nothing, she miserably thought. She was now once again in survival mode. She had to get through this. She had to get through this and rebuild. Red was determined not to be like her mother and have to depend on a drunken abuser when she was older. She would do whatever she had to do now to ensure that her life turned out differently.

Red crawled along and stopped when she reached his feet. Bacon reached in his back pocket and pulled out a piece of paper, then looked down at Red.

"What was that bullshit you said to me before?" he asked.

"What are you talking about?" Red looked up at him with questioning eyes. "Can we talk about this? You acting weird, Bacon—you know this ain't like you."

Laughing at Red's crazy remark, Bacon read aloud in a stentorian voice:

Dear Bacon,

Or, in your case, should I say Dear John? This is the letter you been begging for.

Well, let's see. It would be virtually impossible for you to kick my ass, seeing as how you will be an old and gray bastard when you come home. You dick is so little that I can't believe you ever wear a size 12 shoe. There goes that myth. When I first met you I sized you up real good and I knew the dick was going to be swinging. Boy, was I wrong. I guess that teaches me not to judge a book by its cover, or a dick by its shoe size.

I hope with all the free time on your hands you now realize that I never loved you. As quiet as it was kept, I didn't even like you. Before you got locked up I couldn't even stand the sight of your ugly face, and let's not discuss the revolting sound of your voice.

"Bacon, I told you I—"

He skipped down to the next paragraph and read, " *'Your partner Stan's cum tastes like ice cream in my mouth.'* " He skipped down further. " *'I got your loot, you took the case, now press that bunk and do that muthafuckin' time.'* "

Bacon's hand began to crumple the paper as he read, " *'My new man and I reap all the benefits . . . get you a boyfriend, let him suck your dick and leave me the fuck alone.'* "

Bacon unfastened his pants and allowed them to fall to the floor. "Stan's cum tastes like ice cream, huh?" He grabbed a handful of Red's hair and forced her head to his smelly crotch. "Suck my dick, you dirty bitch."

Red instinctively moved her face away and Bacon knew why. Prior to meeting her at the house, he'd made a run by Foxy's, fucked her real good in her ass and didn't wash his dick afterward. He figured that was something Red could do for him.

"Open up," he sang as he waved his flaccid member in front of her. He caressed the side of her face with his .357 and kept the barrel of the gun right at her temple. "Bitch, I said open up," Bacon grunted through tightly closed teeth and Red knew he wasn't playing with her.

What the fuck am I doing? Red asked herself when she opened her mouth to take him in.

"Bite me and I swear, you're dead," Bacon warned.

Reluctantly, Red began to suck his dick. The taste of it was wretched enough, but the smell almost made her gag. *Got this nigga's nasty-ass dick in my mouth. I gotta get outta here. This nigga gonna kill me. Lord, please help me.*

"Suck it, bitch. Suck my muthafuckin' dick like you sucked Stan's and all them other niggas you had strollin' up in my crib." He angrily shoved his dick farther in her mouth when he emphasized *my crib*.

The more Red sucked the softer his dick seemed to become. Bacon began grinding his groin into her face until the feeling of relief took over his body as he let go of a warm liquid. "Yeah, drink it up, ho," he said as he peed in her mouth.

Red snatched her head back and shouted, "You grimy bastard!"

Bacon hissed at the pleasure of relieving himself but quickly grabbed his dick and finished by aiming the flow of pee on Red's face. Her body had been violated before, but she had never felt like this. She had been forced to suck a nasty, stinky-ass dick and drink urine. Red was even more convinced now that Bacon was crazy and was certain that he was going to kill her.

CHAPTER TWO

*W*hat it taste like?" Bacon grinned at her with a demented look on his face. "It taste better than Stan's cum?"

Bacon loved forcing Red into submission. He wanted her to suck his dick again just on the strength of being able to make her do it but he had other business to take care of.

"Now, get the fuck up!" he shouted.

Red slowly stood up and he motioned for her to get on the bed. "Bacon, I don't—"

"Bitch, I don't wanna fuck yo' piss-drankin' ass. I wanna play a little game with you; now sit down." He patted the bed next to him.

Hesitantly, she did as she was told.

"You heard of the game Russian roulette, right?"

Red nodded.

"Well, I got one bullet in here"—he waved his .357 in front of her—"and you have some choices to make."

Red looked at him and angrily rolled her eyes. Instinctively, Bacon grabbed her hair and jerked her head backward.

"Do that shit again, and I'll break it," Bacon warned, nodding toward her neck. He released her hair when it looked like she checked her attitude. "Now," he continued in a calm tone, "this game is called Life or Death."

Red held his stare through tear-filled eyes. "Why are you doing this to me?"

Bacon cocked his head to the side and stared at her. "After all you did, you got the nerve to ask me that?" He shook his head in disbelief. "That shit was fucked up, but I still love you, ma."

"You sure got a fucked-up way of showing it!" Red spat. She swung at the gun, trying to knock it away.

Bacon grabbed her hair again, only tighter.

"Word on the street had it you were asking about me."

"Asking about you? Huh . . . I don't think so."

Bacon shook his head. "You really think I'm still that same stupid Bacon you knew before he got locked up, huh? You stole from me when I gave you whatever you wanted. You disrespected my house and . . . I should just . . ." Bacon reached toward her throat. He wanted to choke the life out of her, but he stopped. "I can't blame you, Red, for doing what you did. I mean, I was gone for a while, but you got sloppy, and worse, you got greedy. Even before I went in I knew you were on some bullshit, but you were so cool about it, I let that shit slide. But you got sloppy when you figured I wasn't getting out. But surprise," he sang, "I'm back and I got more than you could ever want."

"I don't want you or what you have, Bacon."

Instantly, Bacon let Red's hair go and gently turned her face toward him. "I can give you the world, Red. Anything you want . . . it's yours."

"I don't need you because I have my own," she retorted.

"No, you don't. I know it and so do you."

"You don't know shit, Bacon."

He chuckled. "You really think so?"

"I know so."

"This is gonna be fun," he mumbled under his breath and swiped at his nose. "Just for the record, I know everything."

"You obviously want to tell me something, Bacon, so tell me what you think you know."

"Okay. First of all, you lied."

"About what?" Red knew that whatever he threw out at her, she'd be able to worm her way out of it, so she didn't trip.

"The baby that you claimed was mine wasn't mine."

"That's a lie."

"No, it's not," Bacon replied calmly. "Actually, you didn't know whose it was, Red. Mine or that pretty-ass nigga's, because he thought it was his, too." Red's heart beat faster as she stared at Bacon. He continued. "How you gonna let another nigga nut all up in yo' pussy, then have me go behind him?"

"I ain't make you do shit, Bacon. I ain't wanna fuck you in the first place and you knew that," Red reminded him. She remembered the encounter like it was yesterday. He had her sneak into a restroom, and then he bent her over a toilet and stuck his dick into her dry pussy. The rough, dry sex had given him pleasure but gave her pain. Him cumming inside her had definitely turned her life upside down.

"You may not have wanted to fuck me but you did. The fucked-up thing is, Red, you came to me with some bullshit wanting me to kill someone who killed our baby." Bacon laughed. "Our baby?"

"Yes, our baby . . ." Red started. Why she continued to defend the idea, she didn't know, but she knew that she needed to calm him down.

"Red, you're a ho. Who knows whose baby it was?" Bacon asked with a shrug. "I can't claim what I don't know is mine so I ain't fucking with nobody over it. You should have died when that bastard died."

Red lowered her head.

"Secondly, you stole from me," he continued.

"Bacon, you left me in charge of things. I had to have money to take care of what I needed. That's not stealing."

Bacon became angry at her allegations. "Don't tell me that you didn't rip me off. You not telling me what you're using my money for is stealing. It's not like I would have said no and you know that. You took advantage of a brotha being down thinking I wouldn't find out about it. But you know what? I took back everything that you took from me and then some. The money from Triple Crown, your bank account and the little business you own . . . it's all mine now."

"What you mean, it's all yours now?"

"You don't remember signing the quitclaim deed?" He shoved the papers in her face. "Same shit you did to me, Red, I did it to you."

Red thought about what she had just been told and her fist flew at him. "How the fuck you gon' take my money out of my fuckin' account . . . take my business . . . you dirty bastard!"

Bacon blocked her blows.

"How the fuck you do that to *me*?" he yelled, holding her wrists. "Now you know what the shit feels like. I had to start from rock bottom all because of you." Bacon realized that he was close to breaking her wrists, so he eased his grip. "Now, do you wanna know how you can redeem yourself? This will wipe out your debt and we'll be equal. The prize comes with unlimited money, but it requires loyalty. Loyalty or death, Red, which one do you choose?"

"Fuck you, Bacon! I hope you die, you dirty ugly bastard!"

"A nine-to-five ain't you, Red," Bacon told her, ignoring what she said. "You were made to be wifey. We can go anywhere in the world and start all over, baby. Just me and you. So . . . what's it going to be? Death?" Bacon cocked the gun. "Or loyalty?"

Red realized Bacon was serious. She gulped and hesitated before speaking up in a whisper. "Loyalty."

D...mas got into his car and decided to go to Q's. He ...n for him that he thought would be helpful, plu... ch warrant for the loft. A security camera had vi... mings and goings the night Zeke was killed. He sa... building, then an older woman. Not long after th... n was seen on video, Red appeared. Detective T... d that after Q and the woman left, he saw Zeke e... ing as well. According to the tape, approximately ... assed before Red walked swiftly toward the exit. Later, Q arrived, then shortly afterward the police and the ambulance. Thomas knew Red was hiding something when she'd slipped up and mentioned murder in connection with Zeke's death, but he needed more.

A man as young as Zeke, without any known medical problems . . . for him to die an early death was very suspicious. Now Detective Thomas had proof.

• • •

Bacon and Red arrived at the loft within a half hour. Swiftly, Bacon parked his Range Rover and looked over at Red. She had tears in her eyes.

"Loyalty, remember?" he said to her. "And everything you could possibly want will be yours. No matter how dirty you are, you still wifey material, Red, and on the real, do what I ask and we can charge it to the game, not your heart, feel me? Now come on, let's do the damn thing."

Slowly, Red emerged from the vehicle and walked into the building, heading toward the elevators. Bacon followed behind her, watching her every movement closely. He had to make sure she didn't turn on him. Even though she chose loyalty over death, he wasn't stupid. Red was still a dirty bitch and he didn't put anything past her.

Red ignored the doorman's greeting as she looked at the two elevator cars in front of her. They both seemed to take their own sweet time returning to the main floor after she pushed the button.

Not making it obvious that they were together, Bacon took out his cell phone and began to fidget with it.

Both elevators arrived at the same time, and Red stepped into the first one then turned around as the door began to close. Bacon slid in right before it closed.

"You ready for this?" Bacon asked as the car began to crawl higher to their destination.

Red nodded.

"Let me hear you say it again, Red," Bacon demanded. "What do you choose?"

"Loyalty," Red told him softly. She couldn't believe that she was doing this. She couldn't believe that she was rolling with Bacon once again. Even if it was just until she could escape, five minutes was too long to her. Bacon was scum.

Loyalty is right, Red thought. *Q has done so much for me and I can't forget that. He risked his life for me. If that ain't loyalty, I can't say what is, but Bacon . . . he can give me the life I want, but would he risk his life for me?* She looked at Bacon, who had impaled her with hard eyes. The elevator continued to climb, now almost at its destination.

The ding alerted Red that she'd finally reached her floor. The elevator doors parted slowly and she stepped off with Bacon behind her.

Walking slowly toward the door of her home, Red decided to do something out of the ordinary. *Maybe Q will pick up that something is wrong*, Red hoped. She needed to warn him. *Maybe he'll call the cops or security or grab his gun and save me*, she prayed silently. She needed to give Q a chance but she didn't want him to get caught slipping. Bacon was a grimy-ass killer, and if Q got in the way, she was sure that Bacon would take it to the maximum. Bacon slinked off to the side, out of view, while Red knocked on the front door and rang the bell. Moments later, Q opened it and Red walked in.

"Damn, what you been doin' up in here?" she asked. It smelled like a distillery.

"You . . . I can't believe you would do all of the shit you've done to me, Red," Q slurred, talking with no obvious purpose.

"What are you talking about?"

"I know how you played Kera and your girl Sasha. I know about the pee test you did and you wasn't even pregnant. If you just wanted money, all you had to do was say it, but naw, you decided to play games. Then when your ass did get knocked up, you told me and that nigga Bacon it was ours. You a no-good, scandalous bitch and you ain't never gonna change, Red. You're still dirty."

"Q, you're drunk." Red ignored what he said and tried to escort him to the couch. "You need to lie down."

"I don't need to do shit but tell you to leave." He looked

closely at her. "Get the fuck outta my house and outta my damn life."

"What?"

"You heard what I said, get the fuck OUT!" he yelled loudly then pointed toward the door.

"Look, I don't know what the hell is wrong with you, but you're wrong about what you think you know," she lied. She wasn't going to admit to anything, especially to a drunk: once Q sobered up, he wouldn't remember what was being said now, and Red knew that. "You're obviously angry for some reason. I'm gonna get some clothes and stay at a friend's for a few days."

"A friend? You ain't got no damn friends, Red." Q then mumbled something under his breath that she couldn't understand.

Red marched to the bedroom but came back in less than a minute. Bacon stood silently at the door marveling at the exchange. Q was so drunk that he hadn't even noticed that Bacon was there.

"Q, where's my shit?" Red demanded. Just then, she realized the pungent smell wasn't Q and his drunken state. It was something else. Something much stronger. It was bleach. She ran to the bathroom and let out a bloodcurdling scream when she saw every designer outfit she owned, soaked, destroyed.

"You bitch-ass muthafucka!" she yelled, running out of the bathroom. "How yo' broke ass gonna fuck my shit up?"

"Easy. I'm just doing what you told me to do in Mexico. You told me to keep the clothes, that they were too much of a reminder of me; yo' shit was too much of a reminder of you, so I had to do something with them. Fair enough, isn't it?" Q smirked.

"You broke bastard!"

"Broke?"

"Yeah, broke!" she retorted.

Q walked up on Red and spoke angrily through his teeth. "That's the second time you called me that and it will be your last. See, that's your muthafuckin' problem. I told you I was getting off the damn streets. I grew up, Red. I was trying to come clean so I could build a better life for both of us, but naw, you ain't want that. You still on that kiddie shit. You know what? Get the fuck outta my house and my life, Red. Play your childish games for someone who cares."

Q turned around to walk away.

"Don't turn your back on me," she yelled.

Q continued to walk away.

"Tell me you love me, Q," Red asked through her tears.

He didn't answer her.

"Tell me you love me," she said again, but this time with a hint of panic tinging her voice.

Standing near the front door, Bacon thought, *What the fuck difference does it make if that nigga loves her? Where is this bitch's head at?* He continued to watch, but was ready to bust a cap in both their asses if things didn't work out like he wanted them to.

Q turned around and looked at Red. Drunk and staggering, he managed to speak. "I did love you, Red, but I can't anymore. I can't love anyone as heartless as you. Now get the fuck out!" he ordered and turned around, attempting to trot off to his bedroom.

"*I* love you, baby," a voice whispered. "Do it."

Instantly, Q whirled toward the sound. He saw it was Bacon. "What the fuck are you doing at my house?" As drunk as Q was, he charged at Bacon.

Immediately, Red reached into her oversize Marc Jacobs bag and pulled out the gun that Bacon had given her. The two men stumbled past her and began to tussle, knocking over furniture. Bacon on top of Q, then Q on top of Bacon. Bacon on top of Q again.

Red aimed the gun directly ahead of her and closed her eyes.

Without warning, a loud *POP* rang out and everything in the room went silent.

$\mathcal{T}$he acrid smell from the gunpowder permeated the air and gray smoke wafted through the room. Red's ears rang from the sound of the gunshot, and a tense thickness hung in the atmosphere.

Bacon's mouth fell open in shock. He ran his hand over his body searching for a bullet hole and then closed his eyes for a second. He didn't feel any stinging or burning sensations, but he knew that it could be shock keeping him from feeling those things. His hand felt something wet. He pulled it back and saw blood.

Bacon pulled away from Q and Red watched as Q slumped to the floor.

Trembling, with the warm gun still in her hand, Red's vision shifted from Q to Bacon, and from Bacon to Q. *What did I do?* she wondered. *How could I have shot him? I was aiming for Bacon!*

Red couldn't believe it. She knew that Q took her with all of her faults and still made her his wifey. How could she have shot him just to live the good life with Bacon? What kind of person was she? Was it really worth it? Was money really worth it? Was her survival in these streets really worth Q's life?

Red knew that she didn't want to start all over from scratch again, and Bacon was able to offer her money and the safety and security that came along with having it, but she knew she could have it all without Bacon. The bruises on her body were evidence enough that shooting Bacon would have been in self-defense and Q would have been her witness. Killing Bacon and reclaiming his fortune was how Red wanted to show her loyalty to Q. With Bacon's stacks, they could live the lifestyle they were accustomed to and wouldn't be afraid of tomorrow without money. Quentin Carter deserved that, not Bacon.

Q was broke now; he had stopped hustling. But she also knew that if Bacon were dead, she'd still have access to his money, she'd have her house back and the ill whips that he had. It was easier with him dead—plus, she had visible bruises on her so she could say killing him was in self-defense. She had a choice. A life with money if she chose Bacon, or living broke if she chose Q. Fear had made the decision for her. She was used to living a certain lifestyle, and was afraid of a tomorrow without money. So she chose Bacon. But she knew she'd fucked up when she shot Q.

In shock at what she had just done, Red lowered the smoking gun to her side. Tears ran down her face as she watched him struggle to breathe. Her back was now up against the wall and there was no turning back. Just as she was about to leave the loft, she turned back and looked at Q. His life or hers? She chose to live.

"Where the fuck you think you goin?" Bacon grabbed Red by her arm. "You never lay a nigga out without making sure you took his ass out completely."

• • •

Q lay on the ground in an expanding pool of bright crimson blood. Pain radiated throughout his body and he began to get cold. He tried to focus his eyes, but they continued to roll. He couldn't believe that Red had shot him. Out of all the things she was, a killer she was not. *She couldn't have been trying to shoot me*, he thought. *Maybe she just got scared and the gun went off in her hand. Maybe she meant to fire a warning shot into the air but accidentally shot me.* Whatever it was, Q was certain that Red hadn't meant to shoot him. It had to be an accident, his heart told him, but she wasn't running to him. Why wasn't she on her knees crying and trying to help him? What did it all mean? The smell of blood filled the air and Q couldn't think straight. His thoughts were rushing into his head all at once and were beginning to become incoherent. His mind was rambling.

"Red . . ." he called out faintly.

Red watched the blood slowly seep from Q's body. She wanted to run to him, drop down to her knees and hold him, let him know that she was sorry, that she was there for him and that they could get through this together. She knew that they could. They could just tell the cops that it was an accident, or that Bacon had pulled the trigger. But would Q do it? Could he forgive her for all she had done and lie for her? No matter how much her mind willed her legs to move, they were cemented to that spot as if she were trapped.

"Red . . ." Q called out again, weakly. His eyes fluttered as he reached out toward her. "Help me . . ."

Bacon heard Q calling out her name and it pissed him off even more.

"What the fuck you calling her for, nigga?" Bacon said, then walked over to Q. He crouched down next to him and continued, "She don't give a fuck about you. She had a choice to make and she made it. Her life or yours and you laying here damn near dead." Bacon leaned forward and whispered softly in Q's ear, "I got my pussy back. Red is fucking and sucking me now. When you die, I'm gonna fuck her on top of your grave, nut on the dirt that covers your casket and then I'm gonna piss on your headstone." Bacon looked at Red. "Ain't that right, baby?"

Red refused to answer. She hated the very existence of Bacon and wished she hadn't closed her eyes when she fired the gun.

"Answer me, bitch!" Bacon yelled, making Red jump.

"Yes," she said hesitantly.

Bacon grinned at Red's admission. Q struggled to lift his head up just as Bacon stood.

"Fuck you, you fuckin' maggot!" Q managed to say.

Bacon looked at Q, reared his foot back and kicked him in the face as hard as he could. "Die, bitch-ass nigga." Q's head snapped back and hit the floor hard. He was already weak but the blow to his head knocked him out like a light.

"Bacon!" Red yelled. "Stop it!"

"Shut up, bitch!" Bacon looked at her. "What, you got feelings for this nigga or somethin'?"

"You hit him! You didn't have to hit him!"

"And you didn't have to shoot him," Bacon retorted quickly with a smile, "but you did." He clapped repeatedly, giving her applause. "You follow directions very well in a game, Red, and it's a good thing; otherwise, who knows what the cops would find out?" He walked over to her and pushed some hair out of her face. "You know, in a way I almost want you to get caught up. That way, you can see how fucked-up it is in prison. Especially with no one on the outside looking out for you. No letters, no visits, no nothing. You couldn't even wipe your ass on a piece of paper and send it to me. I'm tempted to let you see how that shit feels. Looking at life with no hope of getting out and no support. You damn lucky you chose loyalty, Red, because since you're loyal to me, now I have to be loyal to you. That's the way it works—or at least, that's the way it's *supposed* to work. You understand now?"

Red looked down at the gun. Her hands were trembling badly and her body was shaking as if she were holding a jackhammer. She not only could feel her heart pounding in her chest, but swore that she could hear it as well. Her hands were so clammy and sweaty it was as if they had been dipped in water. She glanced around the loft and knew that she had to get out of there.

Red stared at Q. Inside, she was screaming for him to get up. She had made a mistake, one that could possibly cost her her life, either behind bars or six feet under. Despite the blood that she saw, she still willed Q to get up and save her from Bacon again. *Just one more time, baby*, she prayed silently. *Just one more time and I swear, I'ma be right.*

"I said, DO YOU UNDERSTAND?" Bacon shouted, bringing Red out of her thoughts of Q.

"Bacon, please!"

"Bacon, please, what?" he asked with a smile. "Please don't tell the cops that you committed murder? Bacon, please don't show me how it feels to go to prison and be shitted on? Bacon, please don't shit on me out here? Or Bacon, please love me and wife me, even though I really don't deserve it?"

Red's heart was racing as if she had just run the Boston Marathon in record time. Angrily, she turned around and trotted toward the door but Bacon was faster and stopped her, grabbing her arm.

"Keep your muthafuckin' hands off me!" Red shot back.

"Or what?" Bacon smiled dementedly. "What you gonna do, Red?"

She lifted the gun and pointed it toward Bacon's face. He grabbed Red's arm but she jerked it away from him. "Don't come any closer because I don't give a fuck anymore!"

"Oh, so you a killer now? Is that what you're saying? That you're a real killer now?" Bacon backed up, held his arms out to his side and taunted Red: "Do it!"

She looked at Q, then back at Bacon, staring at him with pure hatred in her eyes.

"Do it!" Bacon reached out, grabbed her hand that held the gun and pressed the barrel against his forehead. "If you point a gun at me, I swear you better use it and kill me!"

Red began to tremble. She closed her eyes, turned her head away, then squeezed the trigger. Nothing sounded but a big empty *CLICK!* She opened her eyes and kept squeezing the trigger in dismay.

Bacon let out a demented laugh. "You stupid bitch! You think I was gon' give you more than one bullet?"

He grabbed Red's arm again, and she snatched away from him. Then he shoved her against the wall.

"Q!" she cried out instinctively.

"Q?" Bacon asked. He became furious. "Q! Yeah, that nigga saved yo' ass last time, but he can't help you now. How the fuck you gonna be loyal to me but call another nigga's name? Especially *his* ass. What the fuck he gonna do except die?" He pointed toward an unconscious Q, then looked back at Red. "Can't nobody save you from me. You *belong* to me."

Red glanced over at Q and Bacon backhanded her, sending her flying back into the wall again.

"Bastard!" she shouted. Red felt her face swelling up from Bacon's constant abuse.

"Loyalty, Red!" Bacon said, grasping her arm. "You said that you chose loyalty. You lied to me!"

"No, Bacon, I didn't!" Red said, becoming desperate. "Let go, you're hurting me!"

"Naw, Red, I'ma show you what loyalty is all about!"

"I'm loyal, Bacon!" Red lied. She knew that she had fucked

up. Her whole purpose was to get away from him now. She had chosen his money over Q, and now she was regretting it. "I swear! I'm sorry."

Bacon squeezed Red's arm and led her out the loft's front door. "Just walk and look normal!"

"Okay!" Red tried to pry his hand from around her arm. "You're hurting me," she repeated.

"I said, just walk and look normal!" He tightened his grip.

The two of them took the long trek down the stairs and out of the building. On the way to the car Bacon smiled in satisfaction. Red had just tried to kill for him, and only he knew about it. He held the keys to Red's freedom and she was now his forever, to do with as he pleased. But first, he would make sure that she understood that. First, he was going to break her ass down; and by the time he got through with her, she would be begging for his mercy.

CHAPTER FIVE

*D*etective Thomas pulled up to the front of Q's building. Although Q went off on him earlier, Thomas was used to that type of reaction from people who had lost loved ones, but he had to talk to Q about the latest information on Zeke's death. A black Range Rover shot past him as he was opening the door to his vehicle. The passengers inside made him do a double take. They looked vaguely familiar, enough so that he tried to glance at the license plate but he couldn't make out the last three digits because of the vehicle's high rate of speed. The police radio in his vehicle crackled and came alive.

"All units. Please respond to shots fired at 1222 Riverdale," the dispatcher announced. "Repeat. Gunshots at 1222 Riverdale. All available units in the area respond."

Thomas lifted his radio handset. "Dispatch, this is 5721, I'm on scene at 1222 Riverdale."

"Roger, 5721," Dispatch acknowledged. "Use caution. Backup is en route."

"Roger, Dispatch. Out." Thomas hung his handset back on the radio and climbed out of his vehicle. He observed his surroundings. On the outside, everything seemed calm, even serene. That was, until he strolled into the building and was met with nothing but chaos. People were talking loudly in many conversations, giving their recollection of what they'd heard. Heading toward the elevators, he was stopped by a concierge who was at the front desk trying to answer questions from tenants.

"I'm sorry, sir," the concierge told him. "There's an emergency on one of the upper floors and I cannot let you go any further. The authorities are on their way."

"I'm aware of that and it's okay. I'm a detective." Thomas pulled open his coat and displayed his badge, which he had clasped to his belt.

The chatter among the tenants became quiet with the knowledge he was in some type of law enforcement.

"Oh, okay. Thank you, sir," the concierge said.

"Do you know on which floor the shots were fired?" Detective Thomas asked.

"I heard it in one of the lofts," someone shouted out.

"I heard it below me," another person gave their input, "and I live on the twelfth floor."

Other tenants began to say where they heard the shot but the concierge said to Detective Thomas, "We believe it was the top floor, where the lofts are."

"Did you see anyone leave the building?"

"Some did, but most of the tenants and visitors came down here." The concierge nodded toward the crowd. "Others are staying put in their apartments, but they're calling down here every chance they get." Detective Thomas could tell the man was annoyed.

"How many security cameras do you have and where are they located?"

"Cameras are on each floor across from the elevators and the monitors are located in the security office." He pointed down the hallway.

"Good. I'll review the tapes in a minute, but I'll need you to stick around to identify as many people as you can."

"Okay, Detective."

"Backup is on the way, so please let them up when they arrive. As far as the tenants, please have them remain in the lobby so they can give their statements."

"Yes, sir." The concierge nodded again.

Detective Thomas headed toward the elevator. He planned on investigating the call for shots fired but first things first. He had to talk to Q. He pressed the "up" button, and waited for the elevator to arrive. As the door opened, he coolly walked into the elevator, pressed the button for Q's floor and waited as the elevator carried him up to the top floor. He pretty much had things figured out with Zeke's murder. He knew that he shouldn't go on assumption, but things were fitting together very well. Q, however, held the key to make the assumptions plausible and they needed to speak.

Once the elevator doors opened he was met by several nervous tenants standing in the hallway. Many of them pointed down the hall. Detective Thomas stepped out of the elevator and looked in the direction in which they were pointing. It was Q's place. *Shit!* he thought to himself. *First Ezekiel Morrison's murder, now this.*

"They're in there!" a lady said, pointing.

"Yeah, in there!" another man confirmed.

Detective Thomas pulled out his Glock 23 and slowly crept toward Q's front door. He waved his hand toward the tenants gathered in the hall. "Get inside your apartments and lock your door and stay away from it."

The tenants obeyed instantly.

Detective Thomas crept to Q's apartment and found the door slightly ajar. Carefully, he pushed it open and cautiously looked inside to see what he could. A strong odor filled his nostrils, along with the faint smell of gunpowder. With his gun drawn, he edged slowly into the loft.

"Police!" he announced. "Is there anyone in here?"

No answer.

He walked further and saw blood. His adrenaline began pumping.

"Hello?"

No answer.

"Detroit Police Department! Is there anyone in need of assistance?"

Silence.

Detective Thomas tiptoed further into the apartment, letting his weapon lead the way.

"Oh, shit," he said when he saw Q lying on the floor of the living room with a pool of blood around him. His cell phone was in his hand.

Detective Thomas instinctively reached toward his shoulder for his radio, but it wasn't there. He was in plain clothes so he grabbed for his cell phone and called dispatch.

"Dispatch, this is Detective Thomas responding to a call at 1222 Riverdale. There's a gunshot victim. Please send paramedics, ASAP."

Detective Thomas quickly searched the remainder of the apartment, sweeping through the kitchen, bathrooms, then the bedrooms. Finding nothing, he returned to Q and spied the wound in his stomach.

"Please help," Q called out weakly. He began to cough and blood spurted from his mouth.

"Hold on, man," Detective Thomas told Q, looking for something to put pressure on his wound. Just as he reached to take Q's cell phone out of his hand, a voice bellowed out.

"Freeze!" Police officers appeared at the door. "Hands behind your head!"

"I'm a cop!" Thomas shouted. "I'm the one who answered the call."

Paramedics came barreling through the door, bent on doing their job.

"Hands!" one of the officers shouted, not believing what Thomas said. "Let me see your hands!"

Disgusted, Thomas looked at the three officers in the door, guns drawn, and didn't recognize any of them. He cautiously raised his hands and stood while the paramedics tended to Q. "Sir, can you hear me?" he heard one of the paramedics ask. "What's your name, pal?"

"His name is Quentin Carter," Thomas said loudly to the paramedics, then spoke to the officers. "Look, I'ma show you my badge."

"Careful, buddy," one of the officers told him. "No sudden moves."

"I can't believe this shit," Thomas mumbled to himself. He knew the drill, so he slowly reached down onto his belt and pulled out his badge.

Just then a familiar face appeared. It was his partner, Detective Joshua McDonald, and behind him was their boss, Lieutenant Darrell Connelly, who was also a longtime colleague and friend.

"It's okay, boys, lower your weapons," the lieutenant ordered.

The officers followed the command and began searching.

"Hey, wassup, T," Joshua acknowledged, walking up to his partner. They tapped shoulders. "Nigga, I told you I didn't wanna do a lot of work this week," he joked. "What's going on up here?"

"Man, I was coming by to talk to this cat about his boy's case, you know, the one we investigated a while ago, but a call came through over the radio about shots fired and this is the shit I run into." Thomas shook his head.

"Is it clear?" an unknown officer asked. Thomas looked at him and instantly knew he was a rookie. Young, eager, but afraid of the unknown.

"I believe so. I went through real quick so I could get back to the victim," he confirmed, "but you can check it again."

Tense and cautious, the rookie combed the apartment. Detective Thomas made a mental note to stay away from him. He didn't have time to babysit.

As Thomas, Connelly and McDonald continued to talk, the paramedics were quickly trying to stabilize Q. They had IVs running in one arm and were about to intubate him when he grunted and pointed.

"Detective Thomas, I think Mr. Carter is trying to say something," one of the paramedics called out.

When Thomas rushed to his side, Q pointed toward his cell phone. Thomas took the phone and flipped it open. Immediately, he pushed "talk," to get Q's last number called. It went to his voice mail. "Damn, he was checking messages," he said out loud. Then he went to Q's incoming call list. His number was the last one.

Watching Q closely, trying to read his eyes and his hand gestures, Thomas asked, "What are you trying to say? Give me something to go on, man."

Suddenly Q began to grunt, and he coughed up more blood and began choking. Frantically, he pointed toward his cell phone and then the bedroom.

"There's nobody in there," he told Q.

• • •

Q closed his eyes in despair. He was trying to communicate that it was the enemy who slept in his bed, but nobody understood him. His thoughts became entangled and twisted as he was overcome with dizziness from the amount of blood loss.

Red betrayed him to the fullest. Under any other circumstances he would hold his water and take care of her himself, but this was different. He wasn't sure that he would still be around to do it and just in case he wasn't, he wasn't going to let that bitch get away. Or Bacon. Fuck them. Fuck her! He wanted to wring that bitch's neck and he wanted to blow that nigga Bacon's head clean off. But that could happen only if he survived what they had done to him. He had to survive. He couldn't let that dirty bitch get the last laugh.

In one last attempt, Q stretched out his hand toward the bedroom but the blood loss was too much and the pain was too excruciating. He tried to speak again but it was too late. He slid into unconsciousness.

CHAPTER SIX

*B*acon quickly drove his black Range Rover onto the entrance ramp of the freeway once he was certain he wasn't being followed. Turning the radio down, he drove at a steady pace and looked at Red.

"So, how does it feel?"

"How does what feel?" Red snapped, angrily.

"Killing someone. It's your first kill," he told her. "It's powerful, isn't it? You blasted old boy then you turned around and tried to blast me. Yeah," he yelled, "that's the kinda bitch I want by my side! Someone who will kill for her man!"

Red leaned her head against the window and her thoughts ran rampant. She could see herself squeezing the trigger over and over. Each time she heard the gun pop, she shuddered. *What the fuck did I do?* she thought. *This nigga gonna hold this shit over my head and I know he's going to use it to his advantage.* Bacon now held the keys to her future and Red knew it. He was already torturing her with it, and he wasn't going to let it go anytime in the foreseeable future. The only way that she could be free again was if she once again seized control of her own destiny and got away from Bacon. In order to do that, she would have to rid herself of his slimy ass. But how? It surprised Red that all of the thoughts that ran through her mind ended in death, but could she kill again? Was she really becoming a killer like Bacon claimed she was? She knew she was capable of doing dirty shit—but killing someone in cold blood wasn't her MO. Her actions were merely done out of necessity and she reveled in her victims knowing that she, single-handedly, did the dirty shit. If necessity meant ending a life, then so be it.

How in the hell did I miss? Red asked herself while closing her eyes, playing back that moment in time. When Q and Bacon were fighting, Red had actually aimed for Bacon. She figured if Bacon died, she could come up with a scheme to get his money. When she closed her eyes to shoot, Bacon was on top of Q, but when she pulled the trigger, that was when they must have switched places.

As they rode in silence, Red glanced over at Bacon through calculating eyes. *I want this muthafucka dead,* she thought. *Look at his ass grinnin', ole bastard. You ain't gonna control my life and I ain't gonna be your slave, and you definitely ain't holding this shit over my head. You're getting out of my life, permanently, you bitch-ass nigga—by any means necessary.*

Red continued to stare at Bacon while he drove and wondered if she could methodically plan a murder.

Weaving in and out of traffic, Bacon reached over to Red and patted her on her shoulder, hard.

"'Sup, killa," Bacon chimed, taunting and breaking her out of the reverie she was in.

"You make me sick," Red spat.

"Why? That's yo' new name, isn't it? Killa Red."

"Bacon, don't. Stop it, just stop it!"

"Stop what, Red?" Bacon asked. "The truth? Is that what you want to stop? If so, I got bad news for you, sweetheart, you can't stop the truth."

"I didn't—"

"You didn't!" Bacon laughed hysterically. "Yes, you did! You shot that man. Killed him in cold blood, sweetheart."

"If you didn't—"

"If I didn't what? No one made you do it, Red," Bacon told her, cutting her off in mid-sentence. "You did it on your own because you're a self-righteous bitch who shits on muthafuckas if they can't do you any good. That broke-ass nigga tried to fight me because of you. Nigga almost took a bullet over you and you repay him by"—Bacon put his two forefingers together and mocked a shooting motion—"blasting his ass."

Red turned her head in disgust.

"You killed a man, because you want the life of luxury and he couldn't give it to you. You want the life that I can give, but then you fucked up, Red."

"Nigga, fucked up how?" Red looked at him with her lips twisted up in a snarl.

"You pointed the gun at me and pulled the trigger. You know what that's called, Red?"

Red took her eyes off him and looked straight ahead.

Bacon took his right hand off the steering wheel and grabbed Red's jaw. "I said, you know what that's called?"

"What?" Red answered through a constricted jaw, courtesy of Bacon.

"It's called biting the hand that feeds you."

Bacon released her face, exited the freeway and drove along some backstreets until he pulled up to a seedy motel and parked in front of a room that looked like it should be condemned.

Red stole a quick look around the motel and a cold chill ran up her spine like spiders. Prostitutes strolled through the trash-strewn, pothole-filled parking lot, intermixing with the base heads and die-hard crack fiends. A couple of drunks shared the sidewalk with a couple of passed-out junkies. The half-working neon sign at the motel's entrance broadcast to all that the place had vacancies.

It looked like something on a hard-core heavy metal album cover, or a Bram Stoker nightmare. The only things missing were the evil-looking spires, spooky stone towers and frenzied bats flying around. The sound of gunfire erupted a few blocks away.

Bacon turned toward Red and continued. "You know what happens to a bitch that snaps at her master?" Red didn't answer. "She gets disciplined. That bitch gets put in check by her owner. And I own you now, so I gotta make sure that you never snap at my hand again. Now, get the fuck out," he ordered. Red could see the gun in his hand.

"For what, Bacon?" Red asked seriously, looking around. "I'm not going in there. Can we talk about this, please."

"If you don't get out," Bacon said through clenched teeth, as he pulled back the hammer on the pistol, "I swear, Red, I will shoot yo' ass out here and no one would give a shit. Or you can go inside. Which one do you want, because right now, I could give a fuck." *I'ma shoot you, or you can go inside.*

Reluctantly, Red got out of the truck and Bacon exited, too. He chirped the alarm, then walked over to where she stood, clasped her arms forcefully. After mumbling something to the fiends, Bacon pulled her into the dilapidated room. Red scanned the interior. Holes were scattered throughout the plastered walls; a rat scampered in the corner and ran back into one of the holes in the baseboard. She looked upward and saw black mold across the ceiling. Looking straight ahead, she noticed several roaches scurrying across the floor into the bathroom, but what really caught her attention were the duct tape and extension cords lying across the messed-up looking bed.

Before Red could look at Bacon, he backhanded her, sending her flying into the wall.

"You fuckin' bastard!" Red yelled as she scrambled to her feet. She tried to run but Bacon backhanded her again.

"Shut up, bitch!"

Crying, Red dropped to one knee and held her hands to her face. She knew that she was in trouble, big trouble.

Bacon grabbed Red's arm, lifted her up and shoved her into the bathroom.

"What are you doing? Stop!" Red yelled at Bacon as he began to rip her clothes off. Red's first thought was that he was going to rape her. She tried to fight him off but he was much too strong for her.

Bacon grunted and gritted, ripping off the last of her clothing, then shoved Red into the dirty shower and cut the cold water on.

Red's second thought was that he was going to wash any trace of his DNA off her and just shoot her in the shower. Either scenario was a bad one for her.

Bacon shoved a cheap bar of motel soap into her hand. Red dropped it. Bacon backhanded her hard, sending her slamming against the moldy, stained tile wall inside the shower. He picked up the soap again and placed it in her hand. "Hold it in yo' muthafuckin' hand, bitch," he ordered.

Again Red dropped it.

Bacon became furious. He wrapped his hand around her neck, choking her, slapping her with his other hand until blood shot from her lip and her nose.

Just as Bacon had arranged, three of the fiends from outside walked into the musty room. Stumbling over one another, they made their way to the bathroom and looked on. The stench of their body odor filled the air and each of them looked at Red with something in their eyes that scared the shit out of her.

Red broke down in tears.

"Wash your funky ass, Red!" Bacon picked up the soap and slammed it into the palm of her hand.

The male fiend looked on at Red with lusty eyes and an obvious erection protruded from his dirty and torn pants. The females looked on, mumbling to each other what they could do with Red to get their fix.

Crying heavily, Red took the soap and began to wash herself.

"You see this shit right here, Red," Bacon said, pointing to her spectators, "this is what I had to go through. Having to take a shower every day with other muthafuckas watching. But you still got it better than me. I had to take a shower with thirty dicks watching my every move. There wasn't no dropping the soap or throwing it down. You drop the soap, and you get fucked in the ass. Ever get fucked in the ass, Red?"

"If she no do, I can do," the male fiend interjected in heavily accented, broken English.

Red's eyes grew as large as baseballs.

"Get the fuck outta my room," Bacon ordered. The three dregs of society looked at one another, trying to figure out what happened, but they exited the room quickly. "I don't want none of yo' corroded-ass pussy, Red. My dick don't even get hard for you, so you can relax if that's what you're worried about. You still got the smell of that nigga you killed on you. That's what it's about.

"I got other things in store for you. I want you to feel me. I want you to understand where I'm coming from. I want you to walk in my shoes, and see what it's like to have to fend for yourself without any help. Now hurry up and finish," he yelled.

As soon as Red washed the soap off her body, Bacon yanked her out of the shower, cut the water off and shoved her into the room. Forcing her to sit down in an unstable rickety chair, Bacon slapped her once again, just for good measure. Sobbing, Red held her face and turned away.

Bacon smiled with satisfaction. He had her where he wanted her. She was a coward, but that was only because of his physical abuse. For Bacon, that wasn't good enough. He wanted to control her mind without having to resort to violence. He needed to break her down real good and take away her will to resist. He felt that his plan would do just that.

Bacon lifted the extension cords from the bed.

Instinctively, Red got up and began trying to wrestle the cords from Bacon. "Uh-uh, I played your little game, Bacon," she said, breathing heavily. "You ain't gonna hit me with that shit."

Bacon pushed Red back down into the chair by her shoulders and began to tie her legs to it.

"Bacon . . . stop . . ."

She continued to fight and kick, but once her legs were secured, Bacon yanked her hands behind her back and tied them together as well.

"Why are you doing this to me?" Red cried. She felt demeaned and belittled.

"I'm showing you what prison is like when you ain't got no support."

"Bacon, I get the point!"

"Do you, Red? Do you really get the fucking point?"

"Yes!" Red screamed through tears.

"I don't think you do. See, I would have been cool if you would have been straight up from the get-go and told me that you wasn't going to ride with me. If you had told me that you was going to move on, and did it in the beginning, I would have had to respect that. But you played me, Red. And so that means that you played yourself. Everybody you ever fucked over is now going to get they revenge on you. You know how?"

Red lowered her head.

"Don't hold your head down now, bitch. You a cold-blooded killer. Own up to that name. Hold yo' head high!"

Red looked up at him. Malice, hatred and tears clouded her eyes.

"You know how everyone gonna get their revenge on you?" Bacon shouted again.

Red looked at him but didn't respond.

"They're gonna do what they doing right now, just going about they business. Ain't nobody coming for you. Ain't nobody coming to save you and that's because nobody gives a fuck about you. You so fucking shady that the only way people are gon' know you missing is when they ain't got nobody fucking over them. They gon' know you missing when they lives is better. That's a fucking shame . . . a real fucking shame. You done fucked over everybody and now nobody gives a fuck about you. If nobody gives a fuck about you, then you may as well be dead."

Red broke down into full-blown tears at what Bacon had just said. She knew he was right. She had fucked over so many people and had done some real dirty shit in her life. Family, friends, strangers—all had felt the wrath of Red at some time. *My own mother wouldn't miss me*, Red thought to herself. *Sasha is dead; neither Kera nor Terry would even know how to find me. Why would they? I fucked them over so bad*, Red thought hard in her mind. *Nobody would get in their cars to look for me. Nobody would even ask where I was. Everybody would be happy that I'm not around.*

These thoughts devastated her.

"I want you to suffer like I suffered. See what it's like when you ain't got no help and the only person you can rely on is a person who doesn't give a fuck. Just like you did me, you're gonna suffer slow and painful. I'm gonna enjoy this."

Bacon turned to leave, but before he did, a thought hit him. He stepped to the thermostat and turned the heater on as high as it could go. He wanted her to sweat. He wanted her to smell the heat, the sweat, the funk, the piss and the shit that she was soon going to be sitting in—just like jail.

"Enjoy yourself, Red," Bacon said, closing the motel door and locking it.

Red's eyes wandered around the room. It was already growing warm. She had nothing to eat, nothing to drink, just the sound of rats scampering through the walls. She was truly in her own personal living hell.

CHAPTER SEVEN

*C*hass Reed cautiously parked her car about a block away from Quentin's apartment building. Her case defending Terry was over and it was time to leave town, but she couldn't leave without seeing him. As a woman, Chass understood that women did crazy things—especially when men provoked them to do so. She didn't justify Terry's actions but she understood. That was partially the reason she had to see Quentin.

"Why am I doing this?" she asked herself. "Shouldn't I just leave well enough alone?"

Chass had lost out on a future with Quentin because of her decision to further her education, but Red also played a part in their relationship's demise. The small amount of time she and Quentin had spent together recently reminded her of all the good times they'd shared. It brought back feelings that she never thought she'd have again. It was like déjà vu. Chass had fallen in love with him all over again, and now, once more, she had to say good-bye.

Chass grabbed her purse off of the passenger seat and dug inside, retrieving a small compact. Popping the top, she coated the puff with powder and, in a T-shaped motion, wiped her face. After she was finished, she put the pad back on top of the powder and snapped the compact closed. She threw it in her purse, then continued to dig for her lipstick.

Finding it, she pressed the rose color against her lips, coating each lip twice. A couple walked past her car as she puckered her lips. Chass watched as they walked in unison with their hands clasped together. A sad sigh escaped her lips. "That could have been us," she said softly, reminiscing.

A woman in her profession and educational status often found herself alone. It was no secret that women graduated from college at a 2 to 1 ratio over men, and the higher up the education and career ladder they went, the harder it became to find a partner with whom they shared common interests, ideas and goals. Like many other black women in her predicament, Chass had thought about dating outside of her race, and had even gone out to a brunch or two with white colleagues, but the connection just wasn't there. No matter how nice he was, she couldn't date a man who didn't really understand her culture. Even though her friends and family claimed to be open-minded, Chass knew her mother and sisters wouldn't approve of an interracial relationship, her father wouldn't stand for it and her girlfriends and sorority sisters would disown her. There were just too many complications associated with it . . . and then there was Quentin—the old boyfriend option who was also safe.

She and Quentin understood each other, they hailed from similar backgrounds and, most important, they had history. He was smart, even though he wasn't college educated, but she could change that. He definitely had his own swagger and was fine. Her girlfriends would give their approvals. Chass could see herself spending a good portion of her life with Quentin, and if he went to college, perhaps she would even spend the rest of her life with him. But those were things that she would have to think about later. Right now she had a more pressing matter at hand, and that was to tell the man she loved good-bye.

Saying good-bye had always been hard for her. Cutting off the ignition, she asked herself, "Can I actually look into his eyes and say good-bye? Can my heart handle telling him how I truly feel? What if he came with me? A change of scenery would do him good, especially getting away from that heifer, Red. She's the reason we're not together but I had him first. He needs to get out of this environment and away from this negativity."

Chass's eyes began to glimmer with a hint of hope as she pumped herself up with plans for the future. "He can go to college in New York, move in with me and we can start a life together." Confidently, Chass stepped out of her car, closed the door and chirped her alarm as she made her way toward Quentin's building.

Women were always making plans of building a future based on what they thought a man felt about them. Was she making the same mistake right now? She wondered. Was she putting thoughts into Quentin's head that weren't there? Was she putting feelings into his heart that really weren't there? Would he grab her by her arms, kiss her passionately and plead with her not to leave? And if he did, what would be her answer? Would he come with her to New York? He had his own apartment, but how would he feel about moving in with her? He wasn't no stay-at-home man. And he definitely wasn't the type to sit on the couch, watch soap operas and live off of a woman. If he felt like he was doing that, he definitely wouldn't come with her. Did Quentin love her, was the question she really wanted the answer to. Did he feel the same way about her as she felt about him?

As Chass got closer, she saw a brigade of police cars, an ambulance and a crime scene van. "What happened?" She stopped and posed the question to a bystander after she squeezed through the crowd.

The bystander shrugged. "I don't know what actually happened but I do know what I heard. You see, I was in my living room about to leave my apartment, you know, then I heard a *pop pop pop*!" The bystander exaggerated loudly, then mimicked a ducking motion. He continued, "Then I got down on the ground fast. I said fuck that, bullets travel, and I wasn't stayin' inside so I took my ass outside." The way he was talking, Chass was certain that he was looking for a starring role on the midday news.

Chass heard the crowd gasp and turned to look toward the building entrance.

"Clear the way! Clear the way!" an officer shouted. The officers who were stationed outside taking people's stories began to herd people to the left and to the right, as paramedics wheeled a stretcher with a body out of the building. Even though the victim had an oxygen mask over his face and other apparatuses attached to his body, Chass could clearly make out who it was. Quentin.

"Oh, my God! Quentin! Please, God, don't let this be happening!" Chass shouted.

"Out of the way, people!" an officer ordered again, shoving her to the right.

Chass grabbed the officer's arm. "Officer, what happened? What happened to—"

"Ma'am, do you live here?" he asked curtly, cutting her off.

"No, but—"

Eyeing her suspiciously, he told her, "I would suggest you stay out of the way, then, or better yet, come back when all of this dies down."

Chass narrowed her eyes at the officer. She didn't like how he cut her off not once, but twice. Not liking his answer, she turned to walk toward the ambulance. A strong grasp pulled her back.

"Where do you think you're going?" the officer asked her.

"I'm going to the hospital with him." She pointed toward the ambulance.

Chass turned to watch as the stretcher with Quentin's body was hoisted up and placed inside the ambulance.

"You know the victim?"

"That's what I was trying to tell you but you kept cutting me off."

The officer took out a small notepad and a pen. "How do you know the victim, Miss . . . ? "

"Reed," Chass answered. "He's—he's my boyfriend." She paused. "Um, I mean my friend. No, we're old friends," she continued to correct herself.

"Well, which one is it?" the officer asked condescendingly. "A friend, an old friend or your boyfriend?"

"What difference does it make?" Chass argued. "What happened to him?"

"I'm sorry, I can't release that information," the officer told her.

"Then point me in the direction of someone who can release that information!" Chass smarted off.

Detective Thomas overheard a commotion while he was talking to his partner. Seeing what was going on, he excused himself by saying, "Let me go handle this." He walked over to Chass and the other officer. "I'll take it from here," he told the officer.

"Good," the officer mumbled under his breath and walked away.

"Ms. Reed," Thomas acknowledged. "So we meet again."

"Yes," she said solemnly. "What happened to Quentin?"

Thomas shrugged. "That's what we're still trying to figure out. Do you know anyone who would want to hurt him or see him dead?"

"Dead? Please don't tell me he's . . ." Chass couldn't bring herself to finish the sentence.

"No, he's not, but if I hadn't come when I did, he probably would be. He was in pretty bad shape when I found him," Detective Thomas admitted.

Chass wiped away some of the tears that had fallen from her eyes.

"Oh, my God, Quentin," she said softly and looked upward. "Please don't take him away from me again."

CHAPTER EIGHT

*D*etective Marquez Nuñez strolled through the crime scene with the coolness of a drifting iceberg. No matter how horrific a crime scene was, nothing seemed to faze him. Actually, the bloodier, the better. Nobody could argue about his skills. He was a very thorough detective and took a no-nonsense approach to solving crimes, but there was one thing that everyone agreed upon.

Standing at five feet even and weighing 120 pounds, Detective Nuñez was an asshole in every sense of the word. He had a short man's complex and was very argumentative. The reason he became a detective was solely because he desired the respect that came with a gun and a badge. Having grown up smaller than average, he got jumped on all the time. Marquez vowed that once he grew up he would never be made a punk of again, and he kept his word.

After high school, he went to the academy and graduated at the top of his class. Once he began street patrol, he requested to partner with anyone who patrolled the most dangerous parts of Detroit. Many people thought he was crazy, but he soon made his mark. Although his arrogant attitude was difficult to work with, his colleagues had to give him his props and gave him the respect due because he took down the hardest and the biggest criminals that many of them wouldn't fuck with. Because of this, he quickly gained respect on the streets and was known as Mr. Officer Nuñez. Fighting someone, busting someone in his mouth or putting a cap in someone's ass was not uncommon for him either, and that was why he loved his job. He had a point to prove and on the streets, he made it loud and clear—he wasn't the one to be fucked with.

Marquez Nuñez had *GQ* looks and the wardrobe to match. He often wore Armani and Kenneth Cole suits. Almost passing as Jon B.'s twin, he kept his wavy black hair cut low in a fade and sported a nicely trimmed goatee that framed his thin lips. Regardless of where he was, inside or out, day or night, he always wore stunna shades. He knew that it gave off a certain mystique about him and he wanted to keep it that way.

Most of his fellow cops wondered how he could maintain the style he had on a detective's salary. It was a department joke that he got his suits from the kids section at Macy's, but nobody ever asked what was up or even joked about it with him. He did his job, they did theirs, and that was that.

"Damn, someone was pissed off," he said to himself, looking at the clothes that were marinating in a bleach-filled tub. Because of his expensive taste, he grimaced when he estimated the value of the clothes to be more than $20,000.

Walking out of the bathroom, he strolled throughout the loft while the crime scene technicians did their job. He could sense that his mere presence made things tense, but he didn't care. He was there for a reason and he wasn't leaving until he proved that his theory was correct.

Twenty minutes later, he ended back in the living room and stood by the bloodstain now soaked into the carpet.

Did a woman actually do this? he asked himself. *Look at all the furniture turned over. I don't know many women who fight like that, but looking at the stuff that's destroyed, it could be.* Many thoughts ran through his head.

Deep in thought, he was pulled from his reverie and his eyes darted to the left as footsteps rapidly approached him.

"Well, well, if it isn't the pride of muthafuckin' Puerto Rico!" Detective Joshua McDonald acknowledged with an inquisitive smile.

"That's right, my nigga, and don't fuckin' forget it," Detective Nuñez confirmed, strolling up to him and shaking his hand.

Detective McDonald couldn't stand the Puerto Rican Columbo as a person, but he had to give him props when it came down to his job. They both watched as the crime scene technicians took samples of various fibers and bagged them, dusted for fingerprints, took pictures and tried to reenact what could have happened.

"So what brings you here?" McDonald asked.

"Um . . . just curious," Nuñez remarked with a sly smile.

"Curious, huh?" McDonald inquired with a raised eyebrow. "Don't bullshit a bullshitter, Nuñez. Internal Affairs don't just show up because they're curious."

Detective Nuñez didn't acknowledge his remark. Instead, he asked, "Get anything from the people downstairs? Anyone see anything?"

"No. Most of them gave the same story. Just heard something and got the fuck out."

"Punks," Nuñez replied.

The two men shared a laugh.

"The person who made the call . . . do you know who it was or where they could be? I'd like to ask a few questions."

"Thomas made the call," McDonald confirmed and went on to explain, "He called for backup and EMT when he found the victim."

"Yeah." Nuñez looked around, then spoke again. "Thomas, huh? Why was he here?"

McDonald shrugged. "Not sure, but from the looks of it, if he didn't come when he did, this would be a murder scene instead of attempted homicide."

Detective Nuñez paced slowly. He noticed that everyone seemed to have slowed down doing what they were doing, trying to listen to his conversation. Everyone knew that when he was around, something was bound to pop off. This time, it was just a matter of what. He walked back to McDonald and looked up at him.

"I have a question."

"What's that?"

"You and Thomas are partners, correct?"

"Yes."

"Well, why was he here without you?"

McDonald looked at Nuñez. He knew something wasn't right. "Man, what's going on in that little mind of yours?"

Fixing his eyes on McDonald, not liking the "little" comment, he answered harshly, "Answer my question."

Before McDonald could open his mouth to speak, Nuñez curtly cut him off. "You don't know what the fuck he was doing here. This is why I'm IA and you're a street detective, Detective." Nuñez looked around and saw the overanxious rookie who had been scouring the scene for the past hour. "Ey," he called out, "go find Detective Thomas and tell him to come see me."

Happy to take an order, the rookie scurried away.

• • •

Detective Thomas held Chass's car door open and she slid in. After closing it, he took out one of his business cards from his wallet and wrote down his cell and home numbers.

"If you need to get in touch with me, you don't have to call the station. You can call me anytime," he told her, handing her the card.

"Thanks." She took it and stuck it inside her cup holder.

"Are you okay to drive?"

"Not really, but I have to get to the hospital. Quentin needs me."

"I promise you, Ms. Reed, we'll find whoever did this and will bring them to justice."

Mechanically, Chass started her engine. "Make sure you find them before I do," she told Detective Thomas. She backed up, put the car into drive and pulled off.

Detective Thomas headed back down the block to the apartment building. He wanted to talk to his partner about what he had learned about Zeke's death and, hopefully, tie it into Q's shooting. Both cases smelled of the beautiful blackbird, Raven, and as soon as he could prove it, she would be arrested for murder and attempted murder . . . if Q survived.

When he walked back into the building, the rookie he had been trying to avoid bumped into him.

"Oh, I'm sorry, Detective Thomas, but you're wanted upstairs. Pronto!" He smiled with a gleam, showing off his pearly whites.

Pronto? Where do they get these kids now? Detective Thomas thought. He walked to the elevator and pushed the "up" button. When the car came, Thomas got on and noticed that the rookie was trying to assert his authority in the lobby. Thomas repeatedly pushed the "close" button on the panel. By the time the young officer turned around, the doors to the elevator car were sealed shut. Thomas didn't want to imagine riding up all those flights with the rookie.

Once the elevator reached its destination, Thomas got off and entered the loft. He saw his partner and walked up to him.

"'Sup, man? You lookin' for me?"

"Aye, man," McDonald acknowledged. "Naw, not me, but that little Puerto Rican muthafucka over there."

Thomas looked around and saw Nuñez in his traditional dark suit and stunna shades.

"Shit! Not that asshole." Thomas ran his hand across his head.

"He's been all up in here asking questions. You know the smell of fresh blood brings that muthafucka out, and he's been crawling up our asses."

"What the fuck for?"

Just then, the rookie barreled through the front door and walked quickly over to Nuñez, who turned around and looked at Thomas and his partner.

"I don't know what kinda shit he's on today," McDonald told him seriously, eyeing Nuñez, "but I don't like how it's smellin'. He's asking too many questions about you."

"Me?"

"Yeah. Let me go get Lieutenant. Something tells me we gonna need backup."

Just when he walked off, Nuñez sang, "Detective Thomas," walking up to him. "I didn't see you come in."

"I'm sure. It's hard to see from down there, isn't it?" Thomas joked.

Nuñez laughed with him. "Got jokes, huh? Well let's see how funny this gets."

"What the hell you doing here, Nuñez?" Thomas asked. "You know IA doesn't get involved unless—"

"Unless there's probable cause of foul play suspected within the force."

"And there is none!"

"I understand you made the call to Dispatch," Nuñez told Thomas.

"What was I supposed to do? Yell out the window until someone came?"

"You made the call from your personal cell phone."

"And?"

"What were you here for?"

"Police business."

"What type of police business?"

"Police business," Thomas repeated in a lower octave than before, "that doesn't concern you."

"Well, what concerns me is that this is the second homicide in this apartment within weeks and you're intimately involved in both."

"How in the hell do you figure that? I'm not intimately involved in anything."

"Ezekiel Morrison and now this? Both in the same apartment and you're assigned to both cases? If that's not intimate, Thomas, I don't know what is."

"So what? I was lead detective in the first case. I am a detective and I was doing my job."

"Okay, so what were you here for?"

"I wanted to talk to Mr. Carter about the Morrison case."

"On Morrison's closed case? Right." Nuñez bobbed his head up and down. "And Mr. Carter just happened to be shot when you arrived?"

"That's right."

"Any idea who did this?"

"Not a clue."

"You know he was a known drug dealer."

"And?"

"Were there any drugs in here when you searched the place?"

"I wasn't looking for drugs."

"What? You knew he was a drug dealer and you didn't search the place for drugs? That's kinda fishy, Thomas. Did you fire your weapon, Detective?"

"What's going on here?" Lieutenant Connelly asked, walking up on the two men with McDonald right beside him. "Nuñez, are you badgering one of my men?"

"No, Lieutenant, I'm simply asking a few questions," Nuñez answered. "When an officer calls from a crime scene, not using his department-issued communication device, it raises questions. Not to mention, Mr. Carter was once a well-known drug dealer and your detective didn't search for drugs." Nuñez paused and looked from one man to the other. "Detective Thomas, are you a drug dealer, too? Is that why you were here, to kill Mr. Carter and take his drugs? You in the game, too?"

"You're way out of line!" Lieutenant Connelly barked.

"You slick-haired muthafucka!" Detective Thomas stepped aggressively toward Nuñez only to be held back by his colleagues.

"Chill, man, he ain't worth it, man," McDonald said.

With a sly smile on his face, Nuñez knew he hit a nerve.

Angry, Detective Thomas backed off.

A cocky Nuñez replied, "I'll need your service weapon for ballistics."

"Whoa!" Lieutenant Connelly interjected. "He said that he didn't fire his weapon and you have no reason to ask for it."

"With all due respect, sir, they all say that," Nuñez countered.

"Fuck this!" Thomas reached toward his side and pulled out

his service weapon and handed it to Detective Nuñez. "I don't have anything to hide."

"We'll see."

"You're a real asshole, you know that?"

"Yeah, I've been told," Nuñez shot back.

"You're completely out of line!" Lieutenant Connelly told Nuñez. "My unit is clean, and I resent your line of questioning. As a matter of fact, this interrogation is over. You want to talk to my detective, I'll make him available to you at the station."

Nuñez closed his notepad. "I'll be in touch, Detective. Don't go too far."

"I'll go as far as I want to go," Thomas retorted.

"I know, Detective," Nuñez told him. "But the question is, just how far are you *willing* to go?"

CHAPTER NINE

*F*or three days, with the heat on full blast, Red slumped over in the chair she was tied to like a rag doll. She tried to move her chair away from the blast of the heat, but after pretty much going nowhere, she decided it was best to conserve her energy. Red sat in three days' worth of her own shit and piss. Not only was she dizzy and light-headed, her mouth was bone-dry and the smell of her fresh urine on top of the old, stale urine almost knocked her out. She was very weak and at times, chills overcame her. Classic signs of dehydration.

Just two days ago, when she was in her right mind, Red knew that no matter how mad Bacon was at her, he wouldn't leave her for too long. Not her. She was wifey. Now, three days had passed and he still hadn't been back. She thought over what he'd said.

Ain't nobody coming for you. Ain't nobody coming to save you and that's because nobody gives a fuck about you. You so fucking shady that the only way people are going to know you missing is when they ain't got nobody fucking them over. They gon' know you missing when they lives is better. That's a fucking shame . . . a real fucking shame. You done fucked over everybody and now nobody gives a fuck about you. If nobody gives a fuck about you, then you may as well be dead.

She was certain that his plan was for her to die, and now she welcomed it.

Two days ago, she thought she was going to lose it. Not because she was hot or because she was sitting in shit and piss. It was because she saw rats the size of small cats nibbling on her Jimmy Choo stilettos. She tried to scoot the chair over and kick at them, but stopped when she almost toppled over. Neither screaming at the top of her lungs nor stomping her foot at the rats fazed them. They were too big to give a damn about what she was doing. She was on *their* territory.

The fluids that escaped Red's body attracted roaches that were the size of playing cards. Not sensing a threat, the rats and roaches battled for space on her body. It was on the second night, when they began to crawl on her face and into her hair, that Red flipped.

The combination of shit, piss and heat made the room smell like a sewer. On the first two days, Red was sweating like an Olympic track star; but on the third day, not too much water escaped her pores. She was hungry, dehydrated and in deep shit no matter how you looked at it. Red's stomach felt like it was touching her back and she didn't know how much longer she would last. By now, her mind was floating on the brink of insanity.

Red's mind raced through her past, like a roller-coaster ride through memory lane. The flashing faces of her mother, Jerome, Blue, Bacon, Catfish, Terry, Sasha, and Kera seemed to be automatic.

"I'll get you," Red mumbled incoherently, then laughed. Her lips stuck together because they were dry. "I'll get you, and you, and you, and you, and you and you, too."

Red wasn't always a dirty bitch. Her life was good until her daddy died. The path of heartache and pain that she traveled had been created by none other than her mother's child-molesting, son-of-a-bitch boyfriend, Jerome. Red looked up to him as a daddy but he certainly didn't treat her like his daughter.

Red's head bobbed to the other side and she thought back to the first time her mother left her alone with him. She remembered her mother putting a drink down on the coffee table just as she was about to leave the house, looking at her as if she would never see her again. She remembered hurt in her eyes but it was something else that at six years old, she couldn't read. She was just an innocent child and Jerome took advantage of that.

As soon as her mother left the house, Jerome was all over her. Red remembered like it was yesterday, his hands inching up her dress until he located her panties. He started massaging the front of them, then moved his hand to her ass.

"No," Red called out in a childlike voice, as the memory seemed real again.

Red remembered him continuing to rub her clit with his thumb over and over again. She remembered struggling against him, but that seemed to turn him on even more. When Jerome licked the side of her face, he stuck his finger inside of her virginal vagina. It hurt like hell. When Red's mother returned he quickly pulled his finger out, hurting her even more, but she was afraid to tell.

"Why didn't you believe me, Mommy?" Red said in a high-pitched voice. She remembered learning in daycare about good and bad touches. What Jerome was doing was bad touches. All of the kids were told to tell their mothers if someone was touching them in a place they weren't comfortable with. When Red told her mother, she ignored her.

"It wasn't supposed to be like that," Red mumbled to herself.

"Mothers are supposed to take up for their daughters. Protect them. Daddy would have kicked his ass."

Red thought about how easy it was for Jerome to get into her panties. At ten years old, he enticed her with material things. Only then did her mother start taking notice. She was wondering why Red got gifts and she didn't.

Red remembered when Jerome presented her with her first pair of diamond earrings.

"Do you want to continue to get nice things?" he asked. He led her to the mirror in the living room and told her to look at herself as he started running his fingers through her hair.

"What are you doing?" she asked.

He took a minute to respond but told her that she was the second most beautiful woman he had ever seen, with her mom being the first.

"Don't you ever let a nigga get something from you for nothing. You so pretty you can make a nigga crawl. Come on, Red," she remembered him begging, sounding like niggas her age while groping at her.

"This is wrong." She tried to twist away.

"If you don't I'll tell your mother you kissed me."

Red knew that her mother would believe him over her. Jerome gave her the most evil smile she had ever seen. They both knew that he had her where he wanted her, so Red went to her bedroom and lay down on the bed.

"Stand up," he told her as he pulled out a Black and Mild, and unzipped her pants and let them fall on the floor.

Jerome kept rubbing on her like she was a grown woman and commenting on how big her breasts were—like a woman's.

He positioned himself on top of her, kissing and touching her. Red felt something on her leg and then he got up and started unbuckling his pants. Jerome stood in front of Red with his underwear on and she noticed something trying to break out of the cotton fabric. It was her first exposure to the penis.

"What you doing?" she asked, confused.

He pulled his dick out and began to stroke it.

Red's eyes got big. "That's too big to go in me."

He ignored Red's words and lay on top of her, kissing her neck at a hurried pace.

"Oh, God," she remembered herself saying. But God didn't help her. He didn't hear her and He never came.

A strange pleasure came over Red's body with Jerome's repeated touches and eventually, a moan escaped her lips. Jerome took that as his sign to move further.

"Can I have sex with you?"

Instead of waiting for her to answer, he spread Red's legs and tried to enter her. When she cried out in pain, he stopped, but she couldn't move.

"It'll be okay," he said softly. "I'll go slow. I'm gon' make it feel real good, okay?" he said in a gentle tone. "I love you, Red." Then he kissed her again. Red was disgusted that she liked those words. When he finally made his way inside her, he kept giving her deep kisses and saying things she wanted to hear. Jerome sickened Red, but she loved the attention so she gave herself to him without reserve.

Red's innocent introduction to sex by a man who couldn't have cared less about her, but who gave her things, turned her into the bitch she was today.

"I'm going to kill you, Jerome!" Red shouted, this time crying without tears falling. "I swear, I'm gonna kill you!" She wanted to pay him back for everything that he had done to her and for everything that he took from her. He took her innocence; he took away her belief in a world that was good. He took away her trust, her smile and her youth. He took away her happiness, and he gave her a hell of a lot of baggage to carry with her for the rest of her life.

"How could you?" Red screamed. "How could you!" She thought of her mother who allowed everything to happen.

As Red grew up, she looked at a man as nothing but a mere trick. Of course, their main thing was to get the pussy, but she made them do tricks before they got the pussy. Having men eating out of her hand was simple for Red because she was a dime, but when she got what she wanted from them, like a piranha, she chewed them up and spit them out. No man was safe in the path of Red's destruction.

She cut off the low-end niggas who had nothing to lose and graduated to the big ballers who had everything to lose. She went from innocent Raven, a gullible, abused girl, to Dirty Red, a bitch who took no shit from nobody and didn't give a fuck about nobody.

Red's memories seemed to fast-forward, and another image was stuck deep in her mind. "Muthafucka!" she shouted as his face began to get clearer. *Bacon,* she thought. He was the one muthafucka she had yet to pay back. *That bastard took my business, my money, the book proceeds, the house, my car . . . he beat me, choked me, made me kill Q, kidnapped me, and now got me tied up in this hot-ass room, sitting in my own shit and piss in a room full of rats and roaches.* She looked down and in her blurry vision, she was able to detect rat bites on her ankles and legs, rat shit in her lap. The clothes that Bacon made her take off were still in the shower, wet; a strong smell of mold and mildew filled the hot air.

"Nigga, you gotta die," she said softly, then broke into sinister laughter. "Bitches," Red cackled. "I'll get all of you hos." Her head tumbled backward. "Stupid-ass Kera, I'll get yo' ass. Ugly-ass Catfish, sorry-ass Blue and crazy-ass Terry. Let me get out of here. I'll get you back one by one."

Red thought about what she had said. If she got out of there, that meant she would have to play Bacon to the fullest. That would mean she would have to appear totally broken in his eyes. Could she play that role and not try to kill him as soon as he freed her, if he came back? She would have to. She had sat in shit and piss for three days so far, and it wasn't going to be for nothing. She would get him in the most supreme way. He was going to suffer like she suffered. He was going to feel pain like she felt pain. She wanted his mind, like he wanted her mind. And she was going to do it. If only that nigga would show back up. And that was the ultimate question. Was Bacon going to come back? Or had he left her to die? Did he mean to starve her to death, and then let the rats and roaches eat her body?

Red began to dry-heave and it hurt. Nothing came up, but something made her look up at the motel ceiling. She hadn't asked for God's help in a long time but she figured that now was as good a time as any to start talking to the Man Upstairs again.

"God, please, please spare my life. I know I haven't done right and I'm sorry but I haven't been done right. I didn't ask for people to hurt me the way they have. Why did You let people hurt me? We're all supposed to be Your children. Why did You abandon me? I need help . . . just a little help, please," she said, crying a tearless cry. Again, she tried to tug at the cords and untie herself but she was too weak. She had been struggling unsuccessfully with the cords for days, and her wrists were now bloody and sore. "Help me!"

CHAPTER TEN

*C*hass gently caressed Quentin's hand, and then gently traced her finger around the IV inserted in the top of it. Tears fell from her eyes for the third time in the last hour. She couldn't believe what she was seeing. She had never seen him helpless. He looked so vulnerable and so weak, it hurt her to see him that way. "One thing is for certain now," she spoke softly, "I will protect you, Quentin. I won't leave your side."

"Oh, my God!" a female voice shrieked. "My baby . . . My precious baby!"

Abruptly, Chass looked up and saw Mrs. Carter standing at the foot of her son's bed in disbelief. She immediately got up to comfort her.

"Everything's going to be all right, Mrs. Carter. I just know it. Quentin is a fighter."

Mrs. Carter looked at the person who was comforting her. Through teary eyes, she asked, "Chass, is that you?"

"Yes, ma'am."

"Where is—"

"I don't know." She knew his mother was inquiring about Red and Chass didn't want to think about her.

"What happened to him?" Mrs. Carter asked, breaking away from Chass's embrace and going to her son's side.

"I'm not sure. All I know is that he was shot at his loft."

"How do you know about all this?"

"Actually, Mrs. Carter, I was coming to see him before I left Detroit. The case that I was working on is over and I wanted to see him before I left."

"He mentioned that he saw you a few times." Mrs. Carter wiped a tear away from her face. "I always liked you, Chass. It was too bad you two didn't stay friends over the years and that . . . that . . . Raven came into the picture."

"It's okay, Mrs. Carter. I'm here now and I'm not leaving him."

Mrs. Carter continued to look at her son and stroke wherever there was not a tube coming out of his body. "I'm here, baby. Mama's here."

"Mrs. Carter," Chass said, "I'm going to leave you alone with Quentin. I think you need some time with him. I'll be out in the waiting room. If the doctors come in, if you wouldn't mind coming to get me, I'd appreciate it."

Just as Chass opened the door, a tall, good-looking African American man wearing a white coat entered the room. He looked at the two women and introduced himself.

"Hello, I'm Dr. Johnson."

Mrs. Carter stood up from Quentin's bedside and spoke. "I'm Quentin's mother, Patricia Carter, and this is Chass Reed . . . Quentin's girlfriend."

Chass made a mental note of that and beamed inside.

"What happened to my son and will he be okay?"

Before answering, Dr. Johnson pulled out his stethoscope and listened to Quentin's heart for a moment. He took out his penlight, flashed the light in both of Quentin's eyes, then looked at the monitors, making note of what he saw. When he was finished, he turned to Mrs. Carter.

"Here's the deal. Your son is now in what we call a double danger zone."

She covered the lower half of her face with her hands and gasped. Instinctively, Chass grasped her for support, each bracing for what could be even worse news.

"Quentin is in a coma right now. He suffered blunt trauma to his rear cranial area, which resulted in major swelling in his occipital lobe. That, along with severe blood loss, sent him into this suspended state. He may be in a coma for a few days, and the danger is that if he does not come out of it during these early days the likelihood of him coming out of it at all is very slim. The second issue is the gunshot wound. The bullet penetrated his abdomen, destroyed his colon and lodged close to his spine. We had to perform a total colectomy, but in his current state we have to wait to try to remove the bullet."

"Why is that, Doctor?" Mrs. Carter asked.

"Well . . . there's no easy way to tell you this," he replied. "We're worried about paralysis. The bullet is dangerously close to his spinal cord. Tests have indicated that he may already be paralyzed. The neurologist who examined him wants to consult with a specialist about whether it's safer to leave the bullet where it is."

"Oh, my God!" Mrs. Carter cried out. "My baby will never walk again?" Tears ran hurriedly down her face while Chass stood, listening, in shock. The man she loved was comatose, possibly paralyzed and had to wear a shit bag for the rest of his life.

"I know that this is difficult for you ladies," Dr. Johnson continued, "but I need to give you all the facts so that we can make some informed choices."

Mrs. Carter nodded for the doctor to continue.

"If he *is* paralyzed, because of where the bullet is lodged, we suspect that it would be from the waist down," the doctor explained. "However, there is a chance that he could be a quadriplegic, especially if we go back in. That's why we're consulting a specialist."

"What are the risks, Doctor?" Chass asked.

"If we leave it in, it could fragment or dislodge; then it could travel to his heart. If we get it, the paralysis that he might experience could be only temporary. The specialist should be here in a day or two."

"A day or two?" both women asked simultaneously.

"Doctor, I'm his mother. Any decisions will have to have my approval. What are his chances if you go back in to get that bullet out without the specialist's consult?" Mrs. Carter said.

"Not as good as I would like them to be, but I would say fifty-fifty. Your son is a young man and a fighter," Dr. Johnson told her.

"And if the surgery goes right, there's still a chance that my baby won't walk again?"

"There's a very good chance." Dr. Johnson nodded. "There's a chance that he can't walk now. I have seen instances where young gunshot victims in his same predicament walk again after things heal."

Mrs. Carter nodded solemnly. "Do it, Doctor. Go ahead and do the surgery. I don't want to risk the chance of the bullet traveling. Whether he can walk again or not, I want my baby alive. I'll take him any way that I can get him."

"I understand." Dr. Johnson nodded. "I'll inform Surgery and get him on the schedule right away." He began to walk away, then turned to face the women again. "Oh, one more thing . . . does your son have a living will?"

"A living will?" Mrs. Carter lifted an eyebrow.

"Yes. It states who can make decisions for him if he's ever

incapacitated and can't make the decisions himself," the doctor explained. "What we need to know is, if things go badly, should any life-sustaining measures be taken?"

Mrs. Carter nodded fervently. She could not believe her ears. Should they bring her baby back to life? Could things really go that badly? She couldn't believe that there was a real possibility that she was spending her last hours with her son.

"Of course, Doctor," she told him. "You do everything in your power to bring my baby out of that operating room alive."

CHAPTER ELEVEN

*I*n the quiet of the night, Kera turned the corner in her banged-up gray station wagon. She prayed the entire trip that her twelve-year-old, sputtering wagon wouldn't cut off on her. She rattled and shook her way down the street, looking for the right address. She had heard where Terry and Mekel were living and she had to see it for herself.

"Out of all the people you could be with, Mekel," she said to herself, still driving, "you chose the heifer who almost killed our baby."

Kera couldn't imagine Terry lying in Mekel's arms again, all hugged up like a real couple, with her son and Terry's kids, looking like a family. Not after all that she and Mekel had been through, not after all that they had shared. She wanted Mekel, and she desperately wanted to build a family with him.

"You're wrong, Mekel," Kera said out loud to herself. Mekel blamed her for their son's condition. "Its not my fault. It's that bitch, Terry. She always wanted to have a baby by you but she couldn't give you one. She was jealous that I gave you one."

Kera did what she felt she had to because Mekel denied her and their baby while she was pregnant. She was hurt, lonely, horny and needed companionship. Sure, she had taken a few drinks, smoked some dro and engaged in risky sexual behavior but she wouldn't have done any of that if Mekel had 'fessed up and claimed her and their child. Kera refused to believe that what she had done had anything to do with her child's diagnosis—fetal alcohol syndrome and the fact that he was mentally disabled way before Terry tried to kidnap him.

Kera drove a little farther and found the address that she was searching for. She turned around and parked on the other side of the street. The rusting gray wagon sputtered to a stop, as if it were protesting being shut off. It shook and combusted a full twenty seconds after the key had been removed from the ignition. Kera sat in the driver's seat, staring evilly at the house.

The house disgusted her because it should have been hers with Mekel. The first thing she wanted to do was bust in there, kick Terry's ass and reclaim her man and her child. Then the thought of picking up a brick and breaking all of the windows ran through her head. Each second that passed, she became angrier. At first she felt that if she just saw Mekel and Terry together, maybe it would help her to let go, but it was just the opposite. "I had to beg you to buy furniture for that fuckin' apartment," she said. "You couldn't even let Terry's memory go. I had to live behind her and shit on the same toilet she had her ass on, but you go out and do this for her?"

Kera hadn't been the same since Mekel broke up with her and ran to Terry's side. She felt like she was losing it; unbeknownst to her, it was the same way Terry had felt when Mekel left her for the chick he cheated with and got pregnant. Kera was also desperate to get a peek at Mekel Jr. Regardless of how the courts portrayed her, she really loved him and wanted to make sure he was okay. The court had awarded custody to Mekel, and severely limited her interaction with the baby because she was the cause of his preventable health problems. It was only because of Mekel she wasn't in prison for child abuse or child endangerment.

Kera tried to focus on the house. From what she could see, it was a modest two-story brick home. Just then the gas lamp in the yard illuminated and Kera became even angrier. "Oh no the hell he didn't!" Kera shouted. In the driveway sat a sleek black GL-Class Mercedes with chrome rims. "That fuckin' bastard even bought that bitch a car!" Kera said in an unstable tone. She started shaking when she saw the yellow "Baby on Board" sign on the back passenger side window.

Angrily, she got out of her car and slammed the door. *This bitch is living the life that I should have had with my man!* Kera's heart started racing and her breathing became heavy. Not caring who saw her, she marched across the street and started up the walkway, which was trimmed on both sides with small green shrubbery. Closer to the house were taller evergreen shrubs and flowers surrounded by a decorative retaining wall. Something made her stop and look at the home again, and a sick feeling ran through her stomach. For some reason, the home looked like it was filled with love.

Finally making her way up onto the porch, she wiped away her tears and slowly walked to the right. She came upon a window that was dressed in sheers, so she put her hands up and lightly pressed her head against the glass.

Kera looked through the window and her mouth dropped. *I cannot believe this shit,* she thought. Inside, she saw the most beautiful Blade glass and cherrywood dining room table, with a modest floral arrangement in the middle. The table was surrounded by matching Madie leather chairs. A large, round brass mirror hung on the wall to the right, flanked by two contemporary sconces. There were several contemporary vases, in various

shapes and sizes, with an assortment of arrangements strategi-
cally placed throughout the room.

She walked to the other window and looked in. The dining
room was something out of a magazine. She didn't think that
Terry would have contemporary taste, but she had to admit, it
worked, which pissed her off even more.

"Who the fuck they think they are? The Huxtables or something?" she huffed. That was when she saw Mekel and Terry
enter the living room, happily, with all of the kids.

Kera's heart dropped when she saw that they were playing
with her son. The sight of Terry touching her child nearly made
her go ballistic. Kera examined Terry carefully. She was thinner,
healthier, prettier even. She wasn't wearing makeup; there was a
natural beauty and a natural glow about her. She was wearing
her hair natural, in short neat locks that complemented her apple
shaped face. Terry looked happy. She even looked sane.

Kera looked down at herself and saw the complete opposite.
What had once physically attracted Mekel to her was gone. "She
still ain't me. She can't make you feel like I did," she confirmed,
closing her eyes, remembering how he used to make love to her.
If Kera only knew that near the end of their relationship, Mekel
could only fuck her if he thought about Terry.

She looked in again and she saw Terry place a gentle kiss on
her son's cheek, then she pursed her lips toward Mekel and he
kissed her.

"Oh, my God, oh, my God," Kera said, almost hyperventilat-
ing. She looked around on the porch to find something to bust
out the windows. She wanted to rush inside and kick Terry's ass
and snatch her child away, but then another thought came to
mind. "What if I had a gun? That's all I need to get my baby and
my man back."

Kera tried to hold back the tears, but she couldn't. "I couldn't
even decorate that bitch-ass apartment we had, but you set this

heifer up in a house? I always had her leftovers, you son of a bitch . . . even after I gave you a child! I didn't sign up to be no fucking surrogate mother," Kera said through clenched teeth.

She saw Terry motion for the kids to go with her, and Mekel sat down in the oversize chair. Just when Kera told herself she had seen enough, Terry returned, wearing an eggshell silk nightie with matching panties. Mekel stood up and pulled her close, kissed her passionately. The two slowly collapsed to the floor and Terry climbed on top of an outstretched Mekel and straddled him. He ran his hand beneath her nightie, feeling her breasts, and a smile spread across his face. Terry leaned forward and she and Mekel again kissed passionately.

Kera was transfixed watching them. They exchanged words that she couldn't hear but she was able to read Terry's lips. She told Mekel that she loved him and it destroyed Kera's heart when he said the words back to her. Mekel lifted the nightie over her head and pulled down her panties. Kera had definitely seen enough.

She raced back to her car in tears. That Mekel had told Terry that he loved her hurt more than anything in this world. *How could he just stop loving me?* she wondered. The fact that they were about to make love in a brand-new house was about to drive her to commit homicide or suicide. Kera climbed into her raggedy wagon and screamed, "Mekel, how could you do this to me?" Saliva and tears mixed and ran down her shirt. "I'm the mother of your fuckin' child. Your only child! *I* should be with you, not that whore!"

Kera tried to gain her composure but all sorts of thoughts ran chaotically through her mind. Suddenly a scary calm washed over her. As she started her car and drove off, she looked at the house and spoke.

"If I can't have my baby, you can't, either. Another bitch will never raise my son . . . especially *that* one."

$\mathcal{D}$etective Thomas strolled into Scott Memorial Hospital and rode the elevator to the sixth floor. Still in plain clothes—blue jeans and a sweatshirt—it wouldn't look too obvious what he was doing at the hospital. He had called ahead, so he knew exactly what room to go to.

Arriving at Q's door, he looked through the small window and saw Chass and another woman sitting by Q's bedside.

He opened the door and Chass turned around at the faint sound.

"Hello, Detective," she said, and stood up. He walked to her and gave her a friendly handshake. "How's he doing?" Detective Thomas asked, looking at Q and the two women.

"About the same."

Mrs. Carter looked up. "I'm Mrs. Carter, Quentin's mother. Are you a friend of his?"

"You can say that," Detective Thomas told her. "Actually, I was the first one on the scene and called for help."

"Thank you so much, Detective." Mrs. Carter's words were sincere and he could tell she was grateful.

Detective Thomas nodded.

"Did you find anything at the apartment that could help determine what happened?" Chass asked.

"Everything is being taken to the lab. If there's anything out of the ordinary, they'll find it."

"Detective, I've been meaning to ask you," Chass said. "What were you doing at Quentin's place? I'm an attorney and I know that detectives just don't show up for nothing, so please keep it real with me."

Mrs. Carter looked up at them. "What *were* you doing there, Detective?"

"I needed to speak with Mr. Carter about his friend Ezekiel Morrison."

"Zeke? What about him?" Chass inquired.

"Did you know Mr. Morrison as well?" he asked her.

"Yes, I did." Chass nodded. "We all grew up together and were very close. Zeke's death is how we reconnected again."

"Oh." Detective Thomas relaxed a bit. "Well, maybe you could help me."

"Sure. What can I do?"

"Do you know of anyone who would want to murder Mr. Morrison?"

"Murder?" both women exclaimed.

"If you're thinking my son murdered Zeke, you're wrong!" Mrs. Carter raised her voice. "Those two were best friends . . . like brothers."

"I'm sorry, ma'am. I wasn't making that type of statement. I was just asking if there was anyone who wanted him dead. Did he have any enemies? Did he owe anyone anything? Who would benefit from his death?"

Both women looked at each other and shook their heads in disbelief. "Nobody that I can think of," Mrs. Carter answered. "He was quite the ladies' man but I never heard anything about him doing something to anyone that would make them kill him, or want to."

"I needed to get some information from him about Ezekiel's murder."

"Murder?" Chass stepped forward. "You're saying Zeke was murdered?"

"Excuse me, I meant death," Thomas corrected, knowing that he had slipped up. "I meant to say Ezekiel Morrison's death."

"What kind of questions?" Mrs. Carter asked, growing more suspicious. "Because I can tell you right now myself, my baby wouldn't harm a fly. Especially Ezekiel. Those two were like two peas in a pod growing up. They were practically brothers."

"No, ma'am, that not what I'm saying," Detective Thomas told her. "What I meant was, I know that the two of them were close.

"Your son was the first one on the scene to find Mr. Morrison, so I was just trying to get more information from him."

"What kind of information?" Mrs. Carter asked.

"I needed to talk to him about Mr. Morrison's acquaintances," Detective Thomas explained. He turned to Chass. "You were close with Mr. Morrison. When was the last time you two spoke?"

"I don't know." Chass shrugged. "Maybe the day before his death."

"What did you two talk about?"

Again Chass shrugged. "I don't remember. Nothing important. Just one of those 'we all need to get together' type of conversations."

"Who's we?"

"Me, him and Quentin," she answered.

"Can you think of anyone who would want to do any harm to Mr. Morrison?" Detective Thomas asked again. "Did he mention anything in passing about getting into it with anyone? Anyone at the club, the park, the movie theater? Perhaps over a woman? Anything, anything at all?"

Chass paused and thought back to her and Zeke's last conversation. She shook her head. "No, not that I recall. He seemed happy."

"Happy?"

"Yeah."

"Did he have a new girlfriend?" Detective Thomas asked. "Did he come into some money recently? Anything change in his life that would make him overly joyful?"

Chass smiled. "Not that I know of." She had been to dozens and dozens of depositions and interrogations. This guy was thorough.

"Ezekiel was always a happy young man," Mrs. Carter added.

"Any chance that he would have committed suicide?" Detective Thomas asked.

"Oh God, no!" Mrs. Carter declared, pressing her hand to her chest.

Chass shook her head in agreement with Mrs. Carter. "No, that's not Zeke. He would never do that. He was way too cocky to take his own life."

"Do you know if he took any kind of drugs?" Detective Thomas asked. Knowing that Chass was an attorney, he had to put this bait question out there. She should bite, he figured.

"I doubt it." Chass shook her head. "Last I remembered, he was always about his money and wouldn't throw it away on drugs. Not even weed. Was there a toxicology report?"

Detective Thomas smiled. She'd taken the bait. "Why would you ask that?"

"You're asking if he did drugs; well, a toxicology report would have answered that question for you," Chass told him. "You would know exactly what he had in his system."

"Was he on drugs?" Mrs. Carter asked. "Do you think that he took some drugs and killed himself?"

"These are just standard questions, ma'am," Detective Thomas explained.

"Well, it sounds to me like that's what you're saying," Mrs. Carter continued.

"No, ma'am."

"Are these the kind of questions that you wanted to ask Quentin?" Chass asked him, kicking into attorney mode.

"Pretty much." Detective Thomas nodded.

"Is he a suspect in Zeke's death?"

"No, not at all. I have my theories, but they don't point toward him at all."

Chass nodded and picked up her purse from a nearby table and rifled through it. She pulled out a business card and handed it to the detective. "I'm not sure what you're looking for, Detective, but if Zeke's case isn't completely closed, please consider me Quentin's attorney. I can help you with whatever you may need. Just please make sure that you get in touch with me before you question my client. I want to make sure that I'm present."

"I'll make sure of that," Detective Thomas told her. He turned toward Q. "So, what are the doctors saying?"

"He's in a coma," Mrs. Carter told him. "He could wake up any minute, or not at all. He's going back into surgery tomorrow morning to remove the bullet. If he wakes up, he may never walk again."

Detective Thomas shook his head in disbelief and mumbled, "Damn," under his breath. "I'm sorry, Mrs. Carter . . . Ms. Reed."

"Don't be sorry, just get whoever did this to my son."

"We're working on it." Just as he turned to walk toward the door, he looked at the two women and spoke again.

"Before I go, I just have one last question. Do either of you know Raven Gomez?"

None of them saw the blip on Q's monitor.

"Red?" Mrs. Carter asked.

Again several blips shot across Q's monitor.

"Yes, ma'am, I believe that's what people call her," Detective Thomas told her.

Q's monitors all went off at the same time. The detective, Chass and Mrs. Carter looked on in shock.

"What's happening?" his mother yelled out. "Quick, go get someone!"

Q's heart rate accelerated, his blood pressure rose and his brain activity began to increase. The constant alarms brought several nurses rushing into the room.

"I'm sorry, you'll have to step out of the room!" one of the nurses told them as she ran to Q's bedside.

Another nurse hurriedly escorted them out of the room but before she could go back inside, Mrs. Carter asked, "What's happening?"

"I'm not sure. I'll come out and let you know. Please go to the waiting room. I'll come and get you as soon as I can."

Chass clasped Mrs. Carter's arm and led her to the waiting room. Detective Thomas followed.

Mrs. Carter began praying out loud.

"Do either of you know where I can find Raven Gomez?" asked Detective Thomas suddenly.

Mrs. Carter stopped praying and looked at Chass.

Out of the corner of her eye, Chass saw a flurry of activity close to Q's room. She darted out of the waiting room with Mrs. Carter and the detective close behind her. Hospital staff quickly rushed past them. "Get him to OR 2 stat!" someone yelled.

With tears in their eyes, the women looked at each other. Neither understood what had just happened, or how Red fit into the equation, but the question was on all three of their minds: Why did Quentin react the way he had at the mere mention of Red's name?

Hours later a tired-looking doctor appeared at the entrance to the waiting room. "Family of Carter," he announced. Chass, Mrs. Carter and the detective looked up. Chass saw the expression on his face.

"Oh God, Quentin . . . no!"

$\mathcal{B}$acon opened the door to the motel room. The rush of hot air and the smell of old urine and feces smacked him in the face immediately, forcing him to drop the bag that he held in his hand.

"Goddamn!" he yelled when the stench wafted into his nostrils. The rats jumped off her body as Red sat naked, seemingly lifeless, in the chair he had tied her to.

She was emaciated from her starvation and dehydration, and totally incoherent. Bacon shook his head and walked to where she was seated, stepping carefully to avoid the rats and the shit on the floor.

"You surprised me, Red." He shook his head. "I thought that you would be tougher than this."

Bacon pulled out a long switchblade and cut the extension cords and duct tape from around her hands and feet. Seeing Red like this disgusted him greatly. He had always envisioned her as being almost invincible. She was always feisty and strong and now she looked like a fragile little tattered, unkempt rag doll. She was a mere shell of her former self.

"I just can't believe you, Red," Bacon continued. "All that shit you talked. All that bullshit you wrote in your letter while I was locked down. Let's see." Bacon pulled out the crumpled letter and read from it. " *I hope with all the free time on your hands you now realize that I never loved you. As quiet as it was kept, I didn't even like you. Before you got locked up I couldn't even stand the sight of your ugly face, and let's not discuss the revolting sound of your voice.'* "

"I can't believe you're the same bad-ass, shit-talking bitch who wrote this trash," Bacon told her, "In case you've forgotten, let me remind you of your words again." He skipped down to the next paragraph and read, " *'Your partner Stan's cum tastes like ice cream in my mouth.'* " He skipped down further. " *'I got your loot, you took the case, now press that bunk and do that muthafuckin' time.'* "

Bacon's hand trembled with fury as he read some more. " *'My new man and I reap all the benefits . . . get you a boyfriend, let him suck your dick, and leave me the fuck alone.'* "

"Bacon," Red mumbled.

"What?" he snapped.

"I'm sorry," she said weakly.

"You're sorry?" Bacon laughed. "I'll bet you are sorry now, Red. Who wouldn't be sorry in your position?"

Red's head bobbed up and down, left and right. Her eyes rolled and she was on the verge of blacking out again.

Bacon snapped his fingers, waking her up. "Hey! Wake the fuck up."

Red came back into semiconsciousness. "I'm sorry."

Bacon smiled. *This bitch is totally broken*, he thought. He was glad that she wasn't as big of a bitch as he thought she was, or else breaking her down would have taken a lot longer. He was willing to leave her tied in the motel room for as long as it took to get her mind right.

"Bacon, I'm sorry."

"Yeah, Red, you are sorry," Bacon said coldly. "You're a sorry, cold-hearted bitch. And you know what, Red? Nobody on the streets is even looking for you. Nobody is even asking about you. Nobody misses you, Red. You might as well have keeled over and died. No one cares."

"I know. Only you care," she slurred softly.

Bacon pulled her up but her weak legs caused her to fall to the floor. The stench of her armpits, her stinky pussy and her shitty bottom was overwhelming.

"Goddamn, Red!" Bacon turned away and covered his mouth and nose for a moment. He grabbed her up by her arm and led her into the bathroom and shoved her into the shower then turned on the cold water full blast.

"No!" Red screamed from the shock. She tried to get out when the water finally hit her, and her consciousness tried to kick in. She thought Bacon was going to beat her like he did before, or this time, possibly drown her.

"Stay in there, baby," he told her while holding her in the shower.

The water began to feel good to her and she realized it was what she needed. It was cooling down her body temperature from the heat in the room. It was washing the filth off of her. She opened her mouth and drank incessantly, unable to quench her thirst.

Bacon opened up a bar of motel soap and guided it into her hand. His dick started to rise as he watched her lather her body. The suds and water looked very exciting on Red's skin. She continued to enjoy her shower. The water felt refreshing, revitalizing, rejuvenating. She almost felt alive again.

Red drank more water. It was delicious to her but it did nothing to satisfy her deep hunger pangs. She needed food.

Bacon reached inside the shower and turned off the faucet. It had been a while since Red had been totally naked in front of him. He grabbed the soiled threadbare towel and wrapped it around her body. He helped her out of the shower and she stood worn and broken in his face. Bacon loved what he saw. She was now his mentally. He led her out of the bathroom and to the bed.

"I bought you some clothes." He picked up the bag and pulled out a fresh set of panties and bra, a pair of jeans, a shirt and some sandals. He was certain that she wouldn't be able to walk in heels once they left.

"Thank you, Bacon."

He loved her submissiveness. He loved it so much that he couldn't stop himself from what he was about to do. Bacon laid Red back on the bed and opened up her towel. Her body was a lot thinner but still beautiful.

He unbuckled and unzipped his pants, allowing them to fall to his knees. Bacon pulled his underwear down and his dick sprang free. Stroking it, he kneeled on the bed over Red. He licked his fingers and rubbed her pussy. On the sly he brought his hand to his nose to smell it. He wanted to make sure that she'd washed her pussy really good. Lying on top of her, he began to kiss her face and her neck.

"I want you to remember all of this," he whispered in her ear. "I locked you down, and I freed you. I control your life, Red, remember that."

Red's breathing became heavy. His weight was crushing her, but he took it differently. Bacon slipped his dick up and down the center of her vagina until he felt her opening. Easing himself inside her, he continued to kiss her face. Instinctively, Red's lips met his.

He pushed himself deeper into her pussy, enjoying the feeling of control it gave him. The more he stroked the more her pussy gripped him. Bacon loved that.

"I can always bring you back here, and let you live with the rats. I can let you live sitting in shit and piss for the rest of your life. Is this how you want to live your life, Red? Is this how you want to grow old?"

He thrust deeper into her.

"Answer me, baby," Bacon whispered in her ear.

"No. Not like this," Red told him.

Picking up his pace, Bacon reminded her, "I'm your lifeline. I'm your only hope for survival. It's about choosing to live, or choosing to slowly die in this shithole. So now let me hear it again, Red. Let me hear your choice." On the verge of cumming, he began to fuck her harder.

The choice for Red was clear. The shower had invigorated her. Her mind could think again, but she couldn't let Bacon know that. She had to keep acting incoherent. But he had hit the nail right on the head. She had chosen survival; survival in order to reap revenge on his sorry ass. She hated the fact that he was fucking her. She knew what he was trying to do, but she was going to get even and then some with Mr. Isadore Jefferies, only he didn't know it. She was going to play the role, tell him what he wanted to hear and gain his trust. If she had to act like a bitch who was completely broken down, then that was what she would do. She was determined to get even and fuck his whole world up.

"Let me hear it!" Bacon shouted, about to nut. He grabbed her hair and pulled her head back.

"Yes," Red cried out.

"Yes, what?"

"I choose you," Red said. "I choose to survive."

Just then, Bacon let out the biggest wad of nut that he could produce.

"Goddamn!" he panted as he continued to thrust into her. He wanted all that he had to shoot in Red. "Whew . . ." He exhaled and finally withdrew himself from her. "Go ahead and get dressed," he told her.

Red did as she was told.

She had just completed step one: get out of the motel room alive. And now, she would work on step two: she would play broken and get his trust. And that would open up the way to step three: she was going to make him wish that he were dead.

CHAPTER FOURTEEN

*A*n hour later, Bacon opened the door and led Red into the place that he had for Maria whenever she came to town, a small brownstone on the industrial side of town that he had purchased and had fixed up. He allowed Maria to stay there because he didn't want her at his place, or even knowing where he really stayed. Bacon had pushed Maria away because he could tell that she had started catching feelings for him. Mixing business with pleasure proved too complicated so he relinquished her pleasure principles and kept everything strictly business.

He had made some changes to the place while Red was locked in the motel. He had all of the windows painted with dark paint so it was impossible to look out them. He also had iron bars installed and dead bolts put on all of the doors, basically transforming the place into a prison. There was no phone or any other mechanisms to contact the outside world. The place was virtually an isolation chamber . . .

• • •

Red looked around, taking in her new surroundings. The furnishings were nice, but not lavish. A nice leather sectional was positioned in front of a 52-inch plasma on the wall. A couple of end tables, a stocked bar and some generic pictures on the wall wrapped things up. Red spied a kitchen adjoining the living area, and her stomach grumbled.

"I gotta step out for a minute," Bacon told her. "There's food in the refrigerator and cabinets. You can make you something to eat. There's some clothes for you in the bedroom."

"Thank you," Red said timidly.

"Oh, and just so you know, there is no phone, no Internet, no fax, no nothing," Bacon continued. "Don't even think about trying to contact anybody, and don't even think about leaving."

"Okay." Red nodded in compliance.

Bacon held something up in his hand. "This is the key to the dead bolt." He nodded toward the front door. "That's your only way in and out and I control that. Understood?"

She nodded meekly.

He headed out the door.

"Good riddance, you bastard," Red said when Bacon turned the lock behind him. She wanted to check it to make sure it was truly locked and he was gone but then thought about it. He might hear her fiddling with the doorknob and think that she was trying to escape. Red walked to the windows and examined them. Her eyebrows rose when she saw the burglar bars. Touching the darkness of the glass, she realized that they were painted over. She shook her head in disbelief. She was trapped inside but if push came to shove, she was certain that she could find a way to get out. But right now, there was no need to. There were other pressing matters at hand.

"Nigga, you think I'm broken but you got me fucked up. I'ma

stay real close to yo' ass and bring you down. Just watch, you ugly-ass nigga."

Bacon thought she was broken, and she needed to remain close to him in order to bring him down and get her revenge. He was already trusting her enough to leave her alone. That was going to be his downfall. She smiled.

Red walked into the kitchen and opened up the refrigerator. An unopened pack of sandwich meat was lying in the deli drawer. A jar of Miracle Whip, mustard and some individual cheese slices were also inside. On the counter next to the refrigerator was an unopened loaf of wheat bread. She quickly put the ingredients together and made a turkey sandwich, which she ate in four bites. Her mind told her she was still hungry, but by her not having had food in three days, that one sandwich filled her up.

Walking around the kitchen, a familiar pain struck her in between her legs. She remembered that Bacon had fucked her back at the hotel. She wanted to get his smell off of her, relax in a hot bath and take a long comfortable nap—something she hadn't had in three days.

She made her way into the bathroom and found a Jacuzzi tub; surrounding it were many of the amenities that she was used to. Bubble baths, body salts, loofahs and expensive lotions. She grabbed two thick towels and put them on the towel rack by the tub, then poured some body salts into the tub while the water ran. The dark aqua blue water seemed to bring a serene sense to Red's mind. She just wanted to get in and soak away.

Red climbed into the tub and let out a sigh of relief as she leaned back and turned on the water jets. The hot water felt good to her. It was totally relaxing. Soon, she found herself dozing off into a deep sleep.

When Red awoke, she found that the water had cooled significantly. She didn't know how long she had been asleep, but judging by the temperature of the water, she knew that it had to have been for a while. Her hands and feet were pruned significantly but her body felt totally relaxed. She climbed out of the tub, wrapped a towel around her and headed out of the bathroom.

"Bacon!" she called out.

No answer.

"Bacon!" she said again, this time checking the door. It was still locked. Red walked throughout the apartment and found that she was still alone. She took that as an opportunity to search.

First she went to the kitchen and rifled through the drawers, finding nothing but a few old receipts. She then went to the bedroom, where she found nothing. Red continued to search, but then she came upon a locked door. She jiggled the doorknob again. Then she bent down to peer through the keyhole. Through her limited vision, she saw what could have been an office. Red thought momentarily, then walked to the bedroom. She looked through the closet and saw wire hangers on the rack with clothes hanging on them that Bacon had bought her. Taking one of the hangers, she carefully untwisted it then walked back to the door. Red had never met a lock that she couldn't pick. Sticking the pointed end into the keyhole, she shook the wire around until the lock clicked. Red's heart raced. *What if he comes back while I'm in here?* she thought. *Just hurry up,* she willed herself.

Stepping into the office, Red moved the few pictures that were on the wall, looking for a safe. There was none. She went to the desk and opened up drawers. The first two opened. She rummaged through them, but didn't see anything out of the ordinary. Paper, computer disks, some porn magazines, but that was it. She tried to open the last drawer but it was locked. Again she took the hanger and stuck it into the lock. She continued to shake the pointed edge around, hoping it wouldn't get stuck, then she pulled at the drawer. It opened. Red smiled.

Her eyes opened in curiosity when she saw what looked like important paperwork. She began to read.

"That son of a bitch!" she yelled. She'd thought Bacon was lying about the quitclaim deed to her business but he wasn't. It was in her hand, with her forged signature. Taking a deep breath, she looked at another, smaller, piece of paper. Red became warm when she saw it. It was a withdrawal receipt written against her bank account. "How in the fuck did he get this?" she said.

She held her head back when a face came to mind. "That bitch." She recalled that Kera worked at the bank. Somehow she and Bacon were in cahoots with each other. If it wasn't for Kera, Red wouldn't be in the situation she was in now. She was also the one who sent the letter that she had written to Bacon.

Red threw the papers back into the drawer, slammed the drawer closed and jiggled the lock with the hanger to relock it. Quickly she left the room and was able to lock it back as if she had never been in there. Kera was number two to be dealt with, after Bacon. Red was going to ruin that bitch's life for real and she had an idea just how to do it. Bacon, Terry, Kera and even Sasha had all been plotting against her while she was screwing them and Red didn't like that.

Red heard keys at the front door. It was Bacon returning. She quickly hid the hanger in the back of the closet and awaited his appearance in the bedroom.

"You wanna play games?" Red said quietly. "Let's play."

CHAPTER FIFTEEN

*K*era paced the floor of her apartment in tears. She couldn't believe what she had just seen. Mekel and Terry were living as if they had never been apart and didn't have a care in the world.

She stomped into the bathroom and turned on the faucet so that she could wash her tear-stained face. Her last conversation with Mekel about the baby played in her head over and over. She could hear him say each word all over again, blaming her for Mekel Jr.'s condition when she went to the hospital to talk to him.

"I'm glad to see you," she said as she walked to stand next to him. When she reached out to stroke his arm, Mekel looked at her and twisted his lips. He walked over to the crib, placed his son in it and began to walk out of the door. "Wait, Mekel. Can I talk to you for a minute?"

"You already said enough," she remembered him telling her.

"Look, just hear me out. I was wrong for blaming you for all of this. We can't let Terry's actions come between us."

Mekel looked at her then shook his head in disgust. "It goes back to Terry, huh?"

"Well, yeah."

"You're blaming Terry, but what about you?"

"What about me?"

"The first three months of your pregnancy. Is there something you need to tell me?"

Kera remembered that her mouth flew open but no words came out.

Mekel knew by her reaction she was busted. "This didn't have to be, Kera, but you elected not to take care of yourself. Is this payback because I wasn't by your side during the pregnancy?"

The memory was too hard for Kera to take. She slumped on the floor and began to cry heavily as she put her hand over her heart. She thought back to what Mekel told her.

"No matter how you felt about me and my actions, your first priority as a mother *should have been protecting the baby growing inside of you."*

She remembered he tried to leave the hospital room, but she ran up to him and grabbed him by the shoulder.

"Mekel!" she remembered herself pleading. "Baby, forgive me! Please, forgive me," she cried. She reached inside her oversize bag, pulling out her NIV Bible, and began thumbing through pages. She mouthed the scripture she found, which she memorized, and read to him. "First John, chapter one, verse nine, says, 'If we confess our sins, He is faithful and just and will forgive us our sins and purify us from all unrighteousness.' Baby, let's pray on this. Let's pray that the Lord will deliver and release us from the grasp of the devil." Then she quickly reached in her purse and pulled out a vial. She quickly opened it, and began sprinkling the oil around the room, saying, "Father God, please bless this safe haven and everyone in it with the strength to pull through this crisis." She walked over to the crib and put her finger on the vial and moistened lil'

Mekel's forehead. *"Bless this child, Father God. He is Your disciple. He's here to serve You."*

The loathing look that Mekel gave her spoke volumes. He couldn't take it any longer. He couldn't stand to be near Kera once he learned of her prenatal neglect. "You really need to stop with your holier-than-thou attitude. If you were so holy you wouldn't have abused your body, oh, I'm sorry, you wouldn't have abused the temple that the Lord gave you." Kera's eyes widened at his condescending tone. *"You talking all that stuff about forgiveness. Yeah, I forgave."*

Kera remembered that her heart thumped happily and her eyes shone with a glimmer of hope at his words.

"I forgave Terry and she's coming home." Before Kera's bottom lip could drop any further than it had, Mekel added, *"Don't worry, I'ma take care of what's mine, but you need to go on with your life and get outta my house."* Just as he opened the door to leave, she remembered that he took one last look at her. *"Don't think I don't know that you've been coming here when I'm gone. Stay away from my son, Kera,"* she remembered him threatening. *"Otherwise, I'll be forced to get a restraining order against you. You can get monitored court-ordered visits when he gets out the hospital."*

Kera got up off the floor. She felt sick at the mere memory of how Mekel spoke to her. She was hurt and wanted the pain to go away. Without thinking she reached into her medicine cabinet.

"How could you do this to me, Mekel?" she cried. "If you didn't want a baby, you should have used protection in the first place, you bitch nigga. You're the one that got me pregnant." She spied a razor and grabbed it. "You know he was okay until that bitch tried to kidnap him, so it's not my fault!" she fumed. "Why can't you see that? Why? Why!" she screamed repeatedly.

Moments later, in a calm fit, she looked down. Her eyebrows rose in shock. Blood stained the sink basin. She looked at her arm and noticed multiple razor slashes. Still grasping the razor in her hand, she slit her arm once again, bringing more blood to the surface. The cut felt good to her. It felt like she was relieving herself, opening up her body and allowing her sins to bleed out.

"Please take away my sins, oh Lord."

She closed her red-rimmed, tear-filled eyes and exhaled deeply. The sting from the razor made her feel alive again. Kera imagined that her blood loss was purifying her and making her holy, that the sacrifice she was giving would help heal her child. Kera was determined that she was going to lay hands on her son and heal him in the name of the Lord.

"You'll redeem me, and I will bring my child into Your bosom, Lord. I will lay hands on him in the name of sweet Jesus!" she shouted.

"I'm going to fix everything. Watch. My baby will be healed. Mekel, you won't be mad and you will come back to me," she said. "I know you're only with that bitch Terry just to get back at me, but I know once things are better, you'll come back home."

An eerie calmness crept over Kera and quietly, she put the razor back into her medicine cabinet. She ran cold water over her wounds until they stopped bleeding, then she cleaned up the mess she had made.

Kera walked out of the bathroom and into the kitchen. She opened the refrigerator and pulled out a bottle of wine that she had been saving. She had turned away from alcohol since becoming deeply involved in church; but after one sermon when the preacher talked about Jesus turning water into wine, she decided that it was okay to buy a bottle from the local liquor store for special occasions. This was a special occasion. She knew that she had experienced a breakthrough epiphany from above.

Kera found her corkscrew and pulled the cork out of the bottle. Then she went into the cabinet and grabbed a wineglass and filled it. She took the glass and the bottle back into the living room with her and began to drink.

"Bless this wine, oh Lord. Let it fill me with Your blood and forgive me my sins against You."

Kera quickly gulped her glass of wine and immediately poured herself another glass . . . and another. Soon she found herself feeling flushed and growing warm, so she began to take off her clothing. Off came her top, then her skirt, leaving only her bra and panties. She poured another glass and the warmth running through her body became almost unbearable.

Kera slid from her couch onto the floor and seated herself with her back against the sofa. She reflected on her life, her meeting with Mekel in Vegas, her pregnancy and the birth of her child. She wanted to get up but she was drunk now. "Fuck it," she said when she tried to pour herself another glass. Her hand wasn't steady enough, so she put the bottle up to her lips and took it to the head.

She became quite dizzy and her eyes went from left to right, watching things twirl in the room.

"I'm sorry," she slurred.

She got up. Steady as a drunk on her feet, Kera stumbled, tried to walk, then fell. "You'll come back to me," she mumbled as she crawled to the bathroom. "Watch. You'll come back." At the sink she pulled herself up. The face that looked at her in the mirror on the medicine cabinet was not one that Kera recognized. But she didn't care. She was in pain. Her man was gone. Her child was gone. What else did she have to lose? She opened the cabinet and grabbed the razor blade once again.

"Thank you, Lord!" she slurred loudly.

This time she took the sharp blade and slashed herself across her wrist.

CHAPTER SIXTEEN

*M*rs. Carter and Chass sat quietly by Q's bedside. When the doctor came to alert them that Q's surgery was over and he was in recovery, Chass had thought they had lost him. The doctor assured them that he was alive, but barely, as he clung to life in the ICU. The surgery was touchy—he had coded on the table—but the doctor was able to bring him back. The rest was now up to Q.

The machines beeped and hummed. Then a faint sound resonated through the air.

"Ummm . . ."

Chass stirred from the uneasy nap she had drifted off into.

"Ummm . . ."

Her eyes grew as big as saucers. "Quentin?" She looked at Mrs. Carter, who was asleep in the chair next to her, and shook her. She pointed toward Q. "He's trying to say something."

His mother quickly shot up and stood by his bedside. "Quentin, baby, Quentin." She touched his face. "Can you hear me, baby? It's Mama. Open your eyes."

Both women watched as Q struggled to follow the command he was given. "Quentin," Chass said softly as his eyes fluttered open briefly. Tears hung in her eyes as she watched him look between her and his mother.

"Wha . . . wha happened?" he asked softly. "Where am I?" His throat was still sore and itchy from being intubated. He tried to move and grimaced in pain.

"Don't exert yourself, son," his mother told him. "Lie back down."

The women sat on either side of him. One held his hand, while the other caressed his face, marveling at the fact that he was so close to death but hadn't left them.

"You don't remember?" Chass said gently.

He looked at the two of them, hoping they would tell him.

"You were shot, Quentin," Chass told him.

"Where . . ."

"In your home, baby," his mother added somberly.

He closed his eyes and tried to block out the faint memory that flooded his mind. The machines started beeping rapidly when he thought of Red. He remembered seeing her in the loft, but what happened afterward was a blur.

He raised his shaking hand and pointed a finger toward a pitcher of water resting on a nearby table.

Chass's eyes followed Q's finger. She got up and walked to the table. Pouring him some water, she brought it back to him and held his head while she put the Styrofoam cup up to his lips. Q sipped the water as best he could.

"Thank you," he whispered. His voice was still weak. "How long have I been here?"

"Three days," Chass said. Noticing that he seemed to be struggling, she asked, "What are you doing?"

"I can't feel my legs," Q said desperately, and he tried to move them again.

Both women tried to calm him down. His mother took the lead. "Quentin Carter, stop it. Stop it now! Look at me."

Q stopped protesting and looked at his mother.

"Baby, you've been shot," she told him sternly. "The bullet stopped very close to your spine. They had to go in and get it out."

"Mama, I can't move my legs!" he said as best he could.

Chass's eyes teared up watching Q in this state.

"We know, Quentin," she managed to say. "The doctors told us that as a result of where the bullet landed, you may be paralyzed."

Q laid his head back on his pillow. The women saw a tear escape from under his lids.

"That's not all," Chass told him.

He lay in complete silence, then she continued.

"The bullet destroyed your colon. You have . . ." Chass couldn't bring herself to tell him the rest.

Mrs. Carter rubbed Chass on her back. "It's okay, honey," she told her. "Quentin, you have a colostomy bag." Q didn't respond. "But it's okay, son. We'll get through this." She looked at Chass. "All three of us."

Q opened his eyes and silently mouthed, "Thank you."

Mrs. Carter left the room to get a nurse to alert her that Quentin had awakened. Chass took that time to talk with him further.

"Quentin?"

"Yes." He looked at her and motioned for her to sit next to him. "What's wrong, Chass?"

After an awkward moment of silence, she spoke. "A detective came up here to see you."

"Thomas?" he asked softly.

"Yes, you know him?"

Q nodded.

"Well, he came to ask you about Zeke."

"I told him to kiss my ass."

"What? Why, Quentin?"

"Because he kept asking me a bunch of questions and wasn't doing the shit he was supposed to be doing." Q started to become agitated and the beeping of his monitors started to increase.

"Calm down. I'm just telling you this because you need to know," Chass said.

"Know what?"

"He thinks Zeke was murdered."

"Murdered?"

"Yes, and get this," she said, smacking her lips in disgust. "He was asking about your little girlfriend."

Chass noticed that Q didn't respond, but she did see a look spread across his face that she had never seen before.

"I can't believe she hasn't even been up here. If you were my man, I'd—"

Q raised his hand to stop her from talking.

"What?" she asked.

"Chass, I'm getting tired." He looked at her. "I appreciate your being here, but I want to get some rest and I really don't want to talk about Red."

Dejected, Chass looked at Q. She thought back to why she'd ended up at his apartment. It was to tell him she was leaving but also to let him know how she really felt. She was confused about why he didn't want to talk about Red and acknowledge her absence. It was obvious. Instead, forming her thoughts carefully so as not to piss him off and upset herself further, she told him, "I lost you twice, Quentin, I'm not going to do it again. If you don't want to talk about this, that's fine. I won't pressure you, but I smell a snake—a Red one. If I find out she had anything to do with this"—she pointed at him—"even though I'm an attorney,

I'm not going to the cops. I'm taking matters in my own hands." She reached over and kissed him on the forehead. "I'm going to go, but I'll be back later."

Chass left the room. Looking for Mrs. Carter, she thought, *I swear, if Red had something to do with this, she's going to wish she were dead.*

CHAPTER SEVENTEEN

*T*erry ambled along a corridor of Scott Memorial Hospital, pushing Mekel Jr. in a stroller. She was coming from a CT scan appointment set by the baby's neurologist.

"Terry? Terry, is that you?"

Terry looked around to see who was calling her name.

"Oh my goodness!" Terry spied someone familiar. She stopped and extended her arms. "Chass, how are you?"

The two exchanged a friendly hug.

Chass took in Terry's appearance. The unkempt woman she remembered visiting at the jail was gone. Terry looked healthy, happy and vibrant. She actually had a glow about herself.

"You look great," Chass admitted. "How have things been going for you?"

Terry smiled. "Things have been going good. I'm still in therapy, and still making progress. Each day I feel as if I'm getting stronger."

Chass looked down at the baby in the stroller. "And who is this handsome young man?"

"Aw." Terry looked down, then back at Chass. "This is little Mekel."

Chass's jaw dropped. "You mean the same—"

"Yes," Terry admitted, cutting her off.

Chass knew that Mekel had dropped the charges against Terry and she was under his supervision. With a raised eyebrow, she asked, "Terry, do you think this is a good idea?"

"He's a baby, Chass. I'm a mother. I will never forget what I did and I owned up to what I did. Mekel forgave me and I owe him so much." Terry reached down and stroked the baby's cheek. "One day I'll be able to look back on this as just another small stone in the path of my life's journey."

Chass hugged her again.

"Thank you," Terry told her. "Wow, you keep coming into my life and saving me. God keeps sending you my way. What are you doing here?" Terry asked, turning the conversation back on Chass. "Is everything okay?"

A somber look fell across Chass's face. "No, not really."

"What's wrong?" Terry asked, concerned.

"Quentin is here."

"Quentin?"

"Yes, Quentin Carter. You may know him as Q."

Terry's eyes shot open. "Q? Red's Q?"

Reluctantly, Chass nodded.

"What's wrong with him?"

"He was shot," Chass told her.

"Shot? Q? Oh, shit!"

"I know. I couldn't believe it myself. He almost died."

Terry put her hand up to her mouth.

"Girl, I'm so tired. I haven't really slept in a week."

"You've been up here with him the whole time?"

Chass nodded.

Terry remembered the story Chass shared with her when she was locked up, and she put two and two together. Q was the man Chass lost. She felt bad for the young lawyer because she could relate. "Where's Red?" she asked.

Chass shrugged her shoulders. "No one's seen her."

Terry shook her head. "That bitch is just out for herself," she said out loud. "After all he's done for her, she can't even be by his side when he needs her? That ho is shady, Chass."

"She doesn't need to be here," Chass told Terry. "I can't stand that heifer as it is, just let her show up here."

The two women laughed. Chass didn't look like she would hurt a fly but Terry was certain that she would kick Red's ass. She would pay money to see that.

"Terry, can I ask you a question?"

"Sure."

"What kind of relationship did they have?" Chass needed some type of insight into what kind of person she was dealing with if she and Red ever crossed paths. It was also to figure out whether Quentin would go back to Red, when it was all said and done. She wanted to know if Red had some type of pull on him.

"Well, I don't know what you want to call it," Terry told her. "They have this twisted history together. He's been there for her, but Red always had other dudes waiting. I don't know if she really loved him or if he was just steady and stable for her.

"From what I could tell, he loved her," she continued. "He would do anything for her."

Chass's heart dropped.

"But I think he started peeping the shit she was into. I don't know if he ever confronted her on it all, but . . . all I can say is be careful. Red's really dirty and no telling what she'll do or how far she'll go to get what she wants. She's a conniving bitch."

CHAPTER EIGHTEEN

*T*his neighborhood has really gone down," Bacon said in a disgusted tone as he looked around. It seemed to get worse each time he visited. Once a nice area, it was now an eyesore.

He knocked on the door, each knock getting louder. He hated creeping into the neighborhood but hated it even more when people took too long to answer their damn doors. The neighborhood was so run-down, he didn't want to be a statistic on anyone's front porch.

Foxy opened the door with her baseball bat cocked and ready. When she saw who was standing on her front porch she lowered the bat. "Oh, it's you."

"Damn, what kinda greeting is that?" Bacon smiled. Foxy wore a short satin robe, which draped open, exposing her naked breasts and a pair of boy shorts.

"What do you want, Bacon?" Foxy asked, pulling her robe closed. "It's late."

Trying to look past her, he responded, "Damn, you got company in there or something?"

Foxy turned her lips up in disgust. "It's none of your damn business who I got in here. You don't pay one damn bill up in this shit."

"C'mon, girl," he begged, "let me in."

"For what?" she asked. "It's one o'clock in the morning. After midnight, that's booty call time and I'm tired of being your damn booty call. Shit!"

"You know it ain't like that," he lied. Bacon loved it when Foxy was feisty. That meant the sex would be great. He stepped up and gently shoved his body against hers. Like he knew she would, she resisted, and he pushed past her. "What you got to eat up in this joint?"

"Humpf," Foxy said, turning around to close the door. Bacon swatted her on the ass. "Boy, you betta quit."

"Or what?" Bacon inquired. "You know when it's on it's on and I come ten men strong."

"Whatever." Foxy walked to the kitchen. "All I got is spaghetti, and I was on my period," she joked. "You want some?"

Bacon laughed at her joke. "Yeah, if you can hook that up, I'd be happy."

He sat and watched Foxy bend over and pull the pot of pasta out of the refrigerator. Her strong, long, toned legs turned him on as well as the perfect hump of her ass. She turned around and slammed the pot on the stove. Her robe opened. Bacon's eyes traveled from her legs to her pussy print that was outlined by the boy shorts. His eyes slowly traveled upward to her flat stomach, and her two perfect round breasts. The best that money could buy. Foxy shoveled some of the pasta onto a paper plate and, like a woman with an attitude, tossed it in the microwave on two minutes.

She turned and looked at him while the food was warming.

Bacon stood up and Foxy spied the bulge protruding in his pants. He walked up on her and put her hand on his dick.

"You want some of this, don't you?"

"Fuck you, Bacon."

In a seductive tone, he countered, "Yeah, fuck Bacon."

Foxy used every bit of willpower she had to keep from dropping to her knees right there in the kitchen. A thick, long, black cock drove her crazy. Like she always told her friends, a nigga with a big dick could make her sing the "Star Spangled Banner" naked in the middle of Central Park on a Saturday afternoon in winter.

Bacon grabbed Foxy and turned her around so that her back was toward him. He kissed her neck, lifted the back of her robe and pulled her boy shorts down. Foxy moaned. Her neck was her spot, and Bacon knew it. He kissed her neck and worked his way over to her earlobe and sucked it.

He bent Foxy forward, over the kitchen sink, and then tried to push up inside her.

"Wait a minute," Foxy protested, raising up. "I need some lube."

Bacon pushed Foxy back down. "I don't want no lube. I'ma show you that I come ten men strong."

The microwave beeped. Foxy meekly tried to raise up again, and Bacon pushed her back down. She liked playing this game with him. Although she liked when he fucked her in her pussy, she especially loved how he fucked her in her ass. Having climaxed from the foreplay, Foxy anxiously awaited Bacon forcibly going up in her. She loved how he punished her and got his nut off in a rough way. It made her want to scream for joy.

Bacon opened her up and pushed himself up inside of her. Foxy tensed and gasped for air. Bacon dug up inside of her with deep, hard jabs, causing her to cry out.

"Is it nine or ten?" Bacon asked, thrusting harder.

"Ten!" Foxy shouted, every time he dug deeper. Then she purred, "It's ten . . ." It was feeling good to Foxy and Bacon knew how to hit it just right. She squirmed, trying to reposition herself.

"Uh-uh, get back here."

He pulled Foxy's hands behind her back, holding her in place so she couldn't go anywhere. All she could do was take the punishment that he was dishing out.

"Huh? I can't hear you," Bacon told her.

"It's ten!" Foxy moaned in ecstasy.

Bacon fucked Foxy's ass for the next fifteen minutes until the tightness of her asshole brought the volcanic feeling of hot cum that stirred in his balls, roaring up the shaft, and erupting out of the tip of his dick. Bacon grunted loud and long as he nutted in her ass.

"Whew, shit!" he said after the feeling subsided. He withdrew his dick and Foxy's tight asshole made a *pop* sound. Bacon smiled; it was his asshole and she knew it.

Foxy stood up and turned around. She looked flustered but sexually satisfied. "You go take a shower and I'll warm up your food again."

Bacon winked at her and trotted off.

Ten minutes later, he returned to a plate of spaghetti. "Thanks, babe," he acknowledged and sat down at the kitchen table.

Hoping she could change things between then, Foxy smarted off. "You got me fucking you like you want, fixing you food and shit, bringing it to you at the table. You got me doing wifey shit, and I ain't getting no wifey benefits."

Bacon shoveled a forkful into his mouth. "C'mere, baby," he said, barely audible.

Foxy trotted over to him and Bacon wrapped his arms around her waist. "You are getting wifey benefits. More than you know."

Yeah, nigga, was the look she gave him.

"So what's been up?" Bacon asked, making conversation.

"What you mean?"

"You keep your ear to the streets. What's going on out there?"

Whenever he needed the 411 on the streets, he knew he could count on Foxy to deliver. It wasn't much she didn't hear. It wasn't much she didn't know.

"This damn ghetto got everybody on their toes. People breaking into other folks' houses and you saw all that shit outside." Bacon remembered seeing clothes, broken toys and things that should have been in people's houses outside, like it was supposed to be out there. "People don't have respect for nothing." Foxy smacked her lips, irritably.

"What's the latest gossip? Who doing who and who got got?" Bacon asked.

"Did I tell you about Lando?"

"That's the dude who got shot up at his crib, right?"

"Yeah, over some damn weed, but check this." Foxy leaned toward him as if she were telling him something confidential and didn't want anyone else to hear. "Lando's baby mama had him set up because he was giving her dick away to another chick and wasn't putting it down right with her no more."

Bacon's eyes widened. "Damn, she had him killed because he wasn't fucking her right?"

"Um-huh," Foxy sang. "Then, remember Moesha? She got her ass kicked by Wanda and her man?"

Bacon nodded his head.

"Well, dude is back with Moesha. He got mad because Moesha told Wanda they was fucking."

Bacon shook his head.

"Bitches just scandalous," Foxy confirmed. Silence fell upon them, then Foxy remembered something. "Oh, you know ole boy, Mekel? You know, the one who was messing with that raggedy hooker, Terry? She the one that got all them damn kids and different baby daddies."

Bacon had to remember. She was one of Red's girls. "Oh yeah, what's up with him?"

"Well, he fucked Red's girl, Kera, and got her pregnant—and get this, Terry got so pissed off, when Kera had the baby, she tried to kidnap him from the hospital. But when she almost got caught trying to leave the hospital with him, she dropped the kid on the floor."

Bacon looked at her. "Terry dropped the baby on the floor?"

"Yup, threw him like he was a football."

"Damn, that's fucked up."

"What's even more fucked up is the baby is retarded."

Bacon's eyes popped open.

"But it wasn't because of being dropped."

"What? Why is it retarded then?"

"Because Kera was doing shit she shouldn't have when she was pregnant. Drinking and drugs and shit. I mean, a lot of folks do it, but she musta been doing a whole hell of a lot of them to make her baby retarded."

"Dang," Bacon sang. Then he thought about it. "Kera. You mean saved Kera? The chick who work at the bank, Kera."

"Yup, the one and only. Don't let that saved shit fool you, Bacon."

He couldn't believe what he heard, but that gave him the leeway he needed.

"Damn, so what's up with that Q nigga?"

"Don't know."

Bacon looked at Foxy. "Girl please, you know everything.

How you gonna sit there and tell me you don't know what's going on with him." Bacon wanted to know if the streets had been talking about his shooting. He hadn't heard anything and it had been almost a week since it happened.

"I'm not telling you shit else about him, Bacon. Last time I did, you ended up trying to kill him. That was so fucked up what you tried to do."

"Well . . ." He shrugged. "Why are you trippin' off of that? You fuckin' him, too?"

"No, I ain't fucking him," Foxy told him truthfully. "He's just a good person and you trying to kill him over a bitch who don't give a damn about either of you. Why are you so concerned about Q anyway?"

He shoveled the last bit of spaghetti into his mouth, then got up and threw the plate away.

"No reason, just making conversation, Foxy."

Foxy knew something was up. He never asked about anyone unless it was for a specific reason and he wasn't one just to make conversation. Bacon had too much of an interest in Q, usually was about that scandalous bitch Red, but Foxy noticed he hadn't even bothered to ask about her ass. She decided right then and there that she was going to use her street connections to find out what was going on. She knew that Bacon wasn't going to tell her the truth, but maybe she could gain a little information through pillow talk.

CHAPTER NINETEEN

*W*ith each passing week, Q was getting stronger. He was released to an inpatient rehabilitation unit where he was to undergo physical therapy for the next three to six months.

Q lay back in his bed and tried to remember the shooting. Chass had told him about it, but the memory was somewhat blurred because of his drunken state. He remembered Red pointing a gun at him, but he knew that she wouldn't actually pull the trigger on him. There was something else he was forgetting. He was confused about why Red hadn't been to visit him and the longer she stayed away, the angrier he became. *I'm going to have a limp for the rest of my damn life, and I got this damn shit bag on my side. Fuckin' bitch. I swear, if I ever run into her again, I will—*

Just before Q could finish his thought, Chass walked in.

"Hi, Quentin!" She happily bounced over to where Q was resting and placed a kiss on his forehead. "How you feeling?"

"I'm good. Just waiting for my therapist to come."

She smiled at him.

"What's that smile for?" Q asked.

"Nothing in particular. I'm just happy that you're alive and you're getting better."

Q looked at her and smiled back. "Chass, can I ask you something?"

"Sure."

"The day everything happened, how did you know?"

She looked at him and didn't know if she should tell him. She was enjoying her time with him and wanted to let everything happen as it was supposed to. She remembered having a long speech she was going to give him that day, but she decided against it. Her being with him through all of this should tell him what he needed to know.

"Quentin, can we not talk about that day anymore? I really don't want to think about that—I almost lost you. You're on the road to recovery now. Let's not mess up anything by talking about the past, okay?"

Q looked at her and wondered what she was trying to hide. The silence was thick in the air but then Chass's cell phone rang, granting a reprieve.

She fished around in her bag to find it. "Hello," she said frantically, hoping she hadn't lost the caller.

"Ms. Reed," a voice said.

"Yes?"

"Detective Thomas."

"Oh, hi, Detective."

"How's Mr. Carter?"

"He's doing a lot better." She looked at Q and beamed. "Actually, he's been moved to Scott's rehab facility. He'll be walking again in no time."

"That's great," the detective told her truthfully. He hated to see a young brotha be taken out by nonsense. "Would you mind if I talk to him for a minute? I need to ask him something about that night."

Although she was an attorney, Chass didn't mind him speaking to Q. She was going to help the detective find whoever it was who tried to kill Q and help to prosecute them to the fullest extent of the law. She didn't want Q to know she was in cahoots with the detective, though. This was between him and her.

"You want to talk to Quentin?" she announced to give Q enough time to decide if he wanted to talk to him.

Q shook his head and hand no, but Chass continued, "Sure, I'll put him on the phone."

With his lips turned upward in disgust, Q reluctantly took the phone.

"Hello," he said in a flat tone.

"Mr. Carter. I'm glad to hear you're doing better." Q remained silent. "We're still working on your case but I'm afraid we're coming up with no leads. I'm going to get the surveillance tapes from that night. Once I get them, would you mind going over them with me to see if you notice anything out of the ordinary?"

"Yeah," Q spoke. "When are you trying to come by?"

"In a few days. I'm working on something else but I could probably get to you on Thursday."

"Okay, Detective," Q told him. He handed the phone back to Chass.

Chass spoke to the detective briefly then hung up.

"What did he want?" she asked.

"He wants to bring the surveillance tapes by here and see if I notice anything suspicious."

"You up to it?"

"Guess I'll have to be."

Q's therapist walked into the room. "Are you ready, Mr. Carter?"

Chass noticed she was a young pretty woman. She resembled

Red, only with dark brown hair. She also noticed how Q's eyes lit up upon seeing her and he perked up.

"Yes, I'm ready."

The cute therapist helped Q into his wheelchair and rolled him out the door.

She looks like that bitch, Red. Is he truly over her? Chass wondered.

CHAPTER TWENTY

*K*era looked in the mirror and didn't like what she saw. Her skin had become ashen and flaky. Her hair was brittle and she looked like she was going to unravel at any minute.

She was getting ready for her monitored, court-ordered visitation with baby Mekel and she wanted to look good. She hated that her visits had to be supervised, but if that was what it took to see her son and Mekel again, then that was what she had to do.

Looking down at her wrists, she cringed. She had been cutting herself for some time now. In fact it had become a habit whenever she was stressed. She knew that she could not see her son with visible cuts and scars on her arms, so she opted to wear quarter-length sleeves and cover the fresh wounds with gauze and white tape.

She got into her old station wagon and drove to Terry and Mekel's house and waited for a representative from the courts to show up.

Looking at the house, Kera became angry again. "It should be me up in that bitch," she said to herself.

Just then, a sleek Honda Accord drove up and parked behind her. A white woman was driving. The woman got out and flounced toward Kera's car.

"Kera?" she asked. "I'm Reisa, and I will be supervising your visitation with your son today."

"Great, let's go." Kera got out of the car and headed slowly up the walkway to the front porch.

"Are you okay to do this?" Reisa asked.

"Yes, it's just kind of awkward," Kera replied.

"I understand."

Kera stood in front of the doorbell, counted to three and rang it.

Within moments, Terry opened the door with Mekel Jr. in her arms.

Eyeballing Kera, and only because the social worker was with her, Terry held the door open for both of them. "Come on in."

The ladies stepped inside and were taken aback by the home's splendor.

"Let's go into the great room," Terry said, still carrying lil' Mekel.

The women followed her. They sat down, then the social worker spoke. "Terry," the social worker said, "will you please give Kera her son."

Terry looked at Kera, then back at the baby, who was fully awake. She handed him over to her.

"Be careful." Terry spoke in a motherly tone. "He still doesn't have full control of his neck muscles."

Kera allowed Terry to place her son in her arms and once she had him, she looked at his face tenderly.

"My baby," she sang. She pulled him close to her and hugged

him tightly. Inhaling deeply, she took in his scent, then pulled him away and took a good look at him. He was thriving and growing. Lil' Mekel looked at Kera and his eyes became quizzical. He gave a few heavy breaths and his bottom lip protruded as best it could. Next came a wail that Kera hadn't expected. Startled, she almost dropped him, but Terry and the social worker were there to prevent anything from happening.

Terry caught the baby and took him from Kera. "It's okay," she told the infant, patting his back and walking back and forth.

"Terry, I'm—"

"I don't want to hear it, Kera. You almost dropped him."

Kera noticed how Mekel stopped crying when he was in Terry's arms.

Her heart cried. *My own son doesn't even want anything to do with me anymore,* she said to herself.

Seeing the bond that Terry and her son had, Kera knew she couldn't compete with that.

"I'm ready to go now," she told the social worker.

"Are you sure?" Reisa had noticed the same thing.

"Yes."

Without saying a word to Terry, or even saying good-bye to her son, Kera got up and headed for the front door.

CHAPTER TWENTY-ONE

*R*ed was growing stronger with each passing day. She played the submissive role that Bacon wanted her in and played it well. She fucked and sucked him whenever he wanted as well as whenever she wanted it. Doing what she was told without asking questions gained Bacon's trust more and more. He had moved her from the jail-like confines of the brownstone back into the mansion with him. At first, Bacon still didn't trust her and had cameras monitoring the exterior and interior of the home, but she was so compliant with his wants and needs, he had even taken to turning those off sometimes. He was watching her less and less each day, and giving her more and more freedom. Her plan was working.

This particular day, he returned from handling some business and found Red in the same place he had left her. On the couch, watching TV. He went into the kitchen and grabbed a beer out of the refrigerator. Strolling back into the great room, he walked past Red, sat down next to her on the couch and picked up the remote.

"Wait, I'm watching this!" Red told him.

"Man, the Cavaliers are playing. Don't nobody want to see no Lifetime bullshit!" Bacon told her. "All this bullshit is the same. A nigga done killed his bitch, a nigga done beat his bitch, a bitch done disappeared and got a new identity. Man, you watching this shit like you getting some ideas and shit."

Red laughed.

"You know you can't disappear on me," Bacon told her. "I'll find your ass or let them folks find you."

"Disappear on you? You think anyone else can take care of me the way you do, Bacon? I don't think so and I ain't stupid. I'm here."

"Good muthafuckin' answer. That's what I want to hear."

"It's almost over, Bacon," Red begged. "I want to see how she gets justice."

"Get justice? Why you want to see that?"

"Because it's personal."

"Personal how?"

"If only you knew my story," Red said softly.

Bacon saw that something was bothering her. He reached out and put his arm around her. "What's wrong?"

"My mother's boyfriend Jerome did the same thing to me that this little girl's stepfather did to her," Red told him.

Bacon glanced at the TV and then back to Red. "What are you saying?"

"I was molested when I was a child." Tears fell from her eyes.

"What?" Bacon declared.

Red nodded, and began crying harder. "He forced me to have sex with him for years."

Bacon couldn't believe his ears. "What do you mean he forced you to have sex with him?" He looked at her and waited for an answer.

"He did."

"Why didn't you tell somebody and stop him?"

"I tried to," Red said. "I told my mother. I was a six-year-old girl telling her what happened and she didn't believe me. When I told her again when I was ten—"

"Wait a minute, he did this to you for four years?"

"Yes. But when he started giving me things, that's when she started to take notice. When I got tired of him fucking me, I told her again; and then she told me I had to get out."

"Yo' mama did that?"

"Yes. I grew up being molested, and not thinking that I was worth shit. I grew up thinking that it was my fault, and that I was trash."

Bacon pulled her close. "Stop crying. That shit ain't your fault. You was a kid."

"I was a child."

Bacon shook his head. "Man, that shit is foul."

"That's why I am the way I am. I grew up not being able to trust nobody, not even my mother. And if you can't trust your own mother, who can you trust? I didn't have anybody but myself growing up, Bacon. So I had to look out for myself. It was a survival game."

"Red, you better not be lying to me and making this bullshit up."

"You think I would lie about something like this?" Red asked angrily.

"Why didn't you ever tell me this shit before?"

"How could I?" Red said, sniffling. "What was I supposed to say, 'Hi my name is Raven, and I'm damaged goods'?"

Bacon felt fucked up inside. "Damn, baby, don't say that. You not damaged goods."

"That's how I felt my whole life. That's the secret that I've carried with me all these years. People don't understand. They think that I'm just some dirty bitch out for myself. But the truth is, all my life I grew up without love and trust. I didn't know how to love or commit to something or somebody. All I knew was how to look out for Red."

Bacon nodded. Now he understood her better.

"I'm sorry, Bacon."

"What?" He looked into her eyes. He couldn't believe those words came from her lips and they sounded sincere.

"I'm sorry that I abandoned you when you needed me. I didn't know any better. I ran away because I was still that same scared little girl inside."

Bacon didn't know what to say. She'd hit him where it really hurt. "Damn, Red, you know how to hit a nigga deep." All this time he hadn't really understood Red, or why she was the way she was, but now he did. She couldn't give loyalty and love, because she didn't know it. No one gave it to her as a child. She wasn't fucked up, she was just abused. It would take a real nigga to show her how to love, and how to be a rider for real. And now he was really fucked up, because he had damaged her even worse. He had piled more shit on top of what her mother's boyfriend and her mother had done to her. *Red didn't need to be broken,* he thought. *She needed to be built up and shown love. She ain't never apologized for this before, so I know she being real with me. She looked me in my eyes and apologized.*

Bacon realized she really had a reason for being the way she was. Red had a way of fucking people's heads up, especially niggas that she fucked with. She had the looks to make niggas act a fool over her and now she was fucking him up with her heart. She had opened up to him in a way that he knew she hadn't opened up to anyone else. Bacon marveled at the thought that Red was finally becoming his.

Bacon pulled Red close and wiped her tears away. He kissed her, repeatedly, and she reciprocated by kissing him back. She felt herself lean back on the couch. She wanted him to make love to her. Bacon unbuttoned Red's pants, slid them off and then tossed them on the floor. He pulled her shirt over her head and tossed it to the floor as well.

Breathing heavily, Bacon and Red stripped each other's clothing off until they were completely naked. There was something different between them now. Something that drew them to each other. Instead of roughly entering Red, Bacon held her closely to comfort her, then he gently slid himself inside of her. In slow, rhythmic movements, they enjoyed the feeling that each gave to the other. They made love on the couch and for Bacon, it was the first time.

After it was over, the two showered, got dressed and went back to the couch. Red broke the silence after a few minutes.

"What just happened?" she asked.

"It was different, wasn't it? Better."

Red smiled.

Bacon rose from the couch, walked into the bedroom and returned moments later with a stack of cash. "Here." He handed it to her.

"What's this for?" she asked, looking at the crisp bills.

"Go out and get you some more clothes," Bacon told her. "Get your hair and nails done, and handle your business."

Red looked at him. He was still sitting.

"What are you waiting for?" he asked her.

"I can't go anywhere without you," she reminded him.

Bacon took one long look at Red and spoke sternly. "You go handle your business." He tossed her the car keys. "Do you, ma."

Red smiled. "Thank you, Bacon." Her plan was definitely working. He trusted her enough to let her go out on her own. Red knew that she was his downfall. She was now free to move around and it was now time to accelerate the pace of her plan dramatically. And all it took was a sad story and a little ass.

CHAPTER TWENTY-TWO

*R*ed parked the large Range Rover in a parking space and stepped out. She had on a pair of low-rise dark denim jeans, a fitted black House of Deréon shirt and a pair of her favorite stilettos. Her long hair bounced as she stepped toward the salon.

Walking past a group of men, Red didn't allow herself to get distracted by them trying to holla at her. She was focused on her task at hand involving Bacon, so she also wasn't fooling around and missing her appointment. There was no way she was going to get sidetracked. She and Bacon were going on a trip to Mexico in the morning and she had to look her best.

Three weeks had passed since Bacon had given her more freedom and now she had a standing weekly hair and nail appointment at the salon.

Red was acknowledged with an accolade of greetings when she walked in.

A familiar voice spoke to her, too. She looked over at the

chair of one of the other stylists and saw Terry, who smiled at her.

Despite the fact that Red had taped her confessing to the shit she did to her house and tried to blackmail her, Terry was genuinely happy to see an old familiar face. She had turned her life around completely, and she had even managed to forgive Red for all of her slights. It was because of her therapy that she no longer held grudges, and was able to forgive and forget.

"Hey, Red!" Terry called out.

"Terry, is that you?" Red asked, surprised. Last she knew Terry was in jail for trying to steal Kera's baby. "When did you . . ."

"It's a long story," Terry admitted. "When you have time, we can talk about it." She didn't want to get into her personal life at the salon. She was already the talk of the streets with what she had done, and people were always trying to get the real story from her.

Red recalled how Terry looked the last time she saw her. "Terry, there's something different about you."

"I know," Terry admitted. "I'm happy now."

"That's good. I'm glad."

Just as Red turned to walk away, Terry asked, "How's Q?"

"Q?" Red jumped slightly. The question had taken her by surprise because she hadn't thought about him since that fateful day. Not that she didn't care. It was just a memory she wanted to forget. *It would be this nosy bitch who would ask about him,* Red thought. "What about him?"

"I heard that he got shot."

"Really?" Red feigned shock.

"You didn't know?" Terry asked. "Everyone was talking about it."

"I haven't talked to him in a long time, Terry. We broke up."

"Really? Last I remember, y'all were really tight."

"I'm with Bacon now."

"Bacon? How'd that happen?"

"I had to go where the money was," Red admitted truthfully. Bacon did have money but eventually it was going to be hers . . . without him.

"Girl, you're still crazy." Terry laughed. Red was still Red. She wasn't worried about Q. She made a mental note to let Chass know. "At first I was going to ask if you thought Bacon shot him. You know that nigga ain't wrapped too tight, but since you are with him . . ."

"Girl, please, Bacon can't do nothin' without me knowing where he is at all times," Red lied. She shook her head. "No. How would I know who killed him?"

"K-killed him?" Terry stuttered. "Q's dead?"

Red looked puzzled. She didn't know how to answer that question. "You said he was shot. I just assumed . . ."

"That doesn't mean he's dead."

"I'm sorry, I shouldn't have assumed that, either. I don't know who could have shot him. I'm surprised. He was getting out of the game." Red couldn't believe that Q was still alive.

"Last I heard he was doing better," Terry told her. "Chass said he was in rehab and learning to walk again."

"Chass," Red repeated. When Red embarked upon Q's life, Chass had to go. Q made the decision to be with Red instead of Chass and each woman hated the other. She was fuming that that bitch had snuck in behind her, but she couldn't tip her hand or let any type of emotion show. She would get even with that bitch, too. *Another one to add to my shit list*, Red thought.

Red knew that she would have to go to the rehab joint and see if it were true. So many questions ran through her head. *Oh, my God, Q is really alive? Was he questioned by the police, and if so, what did he tell them? Are they looking for me or did he not tell them anything?* Red wondered. She hadn't been too visible lately, so she was certain that nobody was after her. However, her thoughts turned to a different question. *Is he going to retaliate against me or does he love me that much that he's protecting me now?* There were so many unanswered questions, so many variables and factors into the equation. *I gotta find out what's really going on,* she told herself.

"Well, I hope that he's doing okay," Terry said.

Red nodded in agreement. She decided that she wasn't going to tell Bacon about Q still being alive. It would be one more ace in the hole for her. She couldn't be a murderer if no one died, and if Q wasn't willing to give her up, then Bacon had nothing over her.

Just then, an annoying little sound came from the other side of Terry. Red looked down and saw a car seat with a baby in it.

"Girl, whose baby is that?" Red asked.

"This is Mekel Jr.," Terry told her.

"Mekel Jr.?" Red repeated, shocked. "What are you doing with that baby?"

Terry laughed. She was becoming used to that reaction from everyone.

"Girl, are you insane? Please tell me that you didn't really kidnap that baby!"

"No, Red! Mekel and I are back together and he has custody of him."

"Oh." Red pressed her hand against her chest. "You scared the shit out of me for a minute. I was about to get away from your ass."

Terry laughed, and on cue, the baby let out another strange-sounding wail. Terry exhaled, leaned over and placed a pacifier in his mouth.

"Are you okay?" Red asked, noticing the stressed look on Terry's face.

"Girl, it's hard," Terry admitted. "I love Mekel, and I want to be with him, but it's just hard caring for a special-needs child."

"Special needs?"

Terry nodded. "He was born with fetal alcohol syndrome."

"Girl, get out of here!" Red exclaimed.

Terry nodded. "Miss Bible-thumping Kera was drinking like it was 1999 while she was pregnant," Terry said.

"Damn," Red sang. She looked at the baby, and noticed that he did have a special look about him. "How's Mekel taking it?"

"He's a great father. His son is his life."

"I'll bet it's a lot of stress on you two."

Terry nodded. "It is, but somehow we manage to get through it. Girl, my therapy helps me cope with a lot of shit. Without it, I don't know what I would do."

Red nodded. She was going over to the bank later, and she was going to happily report that she saw Terry with Mekel Jr. She was also going to rub it into that little Bible-thumping wench's face that her child was a retard.

CHAPTER TWENTY-THREE

*Y*ou did very well today, Mr. Carter," his therapist said. "You'll be walking without that walker in no time."

This was the third day that he had seen her and Q looked forward to therapy. It was a nice getaway from Chass but the girl reminded him of Red, too.

"I'm going to take you back to your room," she told him, "so I can get my next patient."

"No, you don't have to do that," he told her. "I want to try to get back to my room by myself. I just have to go down the corridor until I get to the elevator. My room is not that far once I get off."

Liking his determination, the therapist spoke. "Sure, but if you feel tired at all, just stop someone. They will call me."

"Okay, thanks."

Q slowly ambled his way out of the therapy room and found himself on the main floor of the rehab center.

He continued to walk with his walker until he was outside,

where he stood with his face to the clear blue sky. Q took a deep breath, his mouth open as if he were drinking the sun's golden wine while his eyes followed the puffy white clouds lazily floating around.

"Ahhh." He exhaled deeply. It had been a long time since he had breathed fresh air.

He had been thinking about what the detective told him when he called Chass on her cell phone.

"I gotta get that tape," he said to himself as he stood outside the rehabilitation building hospital.

He wasn't that far from his home. Q took two steps and put the walker down. Two steps again, and he leveled the walker. He had to make it to his place before the detective did.

It took him an hour to walk the five blocks to his apartment building. Very exhausted, Q entered the doors of his building.

Natalie, the front desk person, recognized him.

"Mr. Carter? Is that you?"

"Yes, it's me." He slowly walked over to her.

"I'm glad to see you. And you're looking quite well."

Natalie always had a thing for Q. She didn't like to see him with Red and she made it known, but she was merely a clerical worker and Q was out of her league. She was happy to see him, though.

"What are you doing here?"

"Just trying to get some exercise. Came from therapy and now trying to get back into real life, you know."

"Yeah, but you can't overdo it," she told him.

"Hey, Nat, has anyone been in my apartment since I've been in the hospital?"

"I don't think so. The detectives were only here for the first two days, but I think everything is quiet in there. The detective did call and say he wanted to come by and get the videos of that night, though."

"Oh yeah, he did say that. He wanted me to watch them with him. You know, to see if there was anything suspicious going down that night."

"Well, they're right here." She pointed to two tapes. "He'll get them when he comes by."

Q looked at the tapes. "I can take them with me. I know he'll be rolling through to see me. I can keep him from making the stop."

Natalie looked at him. "You sure you can take these?"

"Yes, it's fine. I'll make sure they get in his hands."

Helping Q out, Natalie put the two videotapes in the side flap pockets of his sweatpants.

"Thanks, Natalie," Q told her. "I owe you."

"Just get better."

Q smiled and slowly turned around and started on his journey back to the rehabilitation building. He was anxious to see what was on the tapes before the detective got to them.

Within another hour, Q arrived back at the rehab facility and took another ten minutes to get to his room.

When he got to his floor, he noticed several nurses and other facility personnel walking about frantically.

"Where have you been?" Chass said as she saw Q step off the elevator. "We've been looking all over for you."

"I was outside." He told half the truth.

"For what, Quentin?"

He looked at Chass with a questioning face. "I've been cooped up for what seems like months and I'll be here for another three to six months because of this rehab. I just needed some fresh air. Is that okay?" he asked with an attitude.

Chass was taken aback by how Q spoke to her.

"Quentin, I was only asking a question."

"I know, but just put yourself in my shoes. I needed some space."

Chass looked at him. She was still shocked at how he spoke to her.

"I'm going back to my room," he told her, "and I'm going to get some rest." Q walked away from Chass, leaving her standing there dumbfounded.

When he got to his room, Q was glad that she hadn't followed him. He gave himself twenty minutes to make sure she was gone. When he was certain she wasn't going to barge in on him, he took one of the tapes out of his pants leg and popped it into his VCR/DVD combo.

Fast-forwarding it, he saw what looked like Red entering the building, and then a man. Red got into the elevator by herself, but the man got in at the last minute. Fast-forwarding even more, Q had to stop the tape and rewind. He pressed "play" again. His eyebrows shot up when he saw Red coming out of the stairwell, with a man forcing her out of the building.

"Maybe the shooting wasn't in cold blood," he said to himself. "Maybe she was forced to do this. Damn, Red . . ."

CHAPTER TWENTY-FOUR

*W*aiting to board the plane to Mexico, Bacon thought about how far he had come up since Red left him with nothing. He was now rolling stronger than ever. The pure Black Tar heroin that he received from Mexico put him as the front man in the streets. He had more and more hustlers coming to him for the product, so many that he almost couldn't keep up with demand. Bacon, along with Red, traveled to Mexico twice a month to see his connect, Juan. Seeing just how big Black Tar was, he wanted to become a major distributor and Juan was just the man to help. He needed to get Juan on board with his plan. Juan was the biggest supplier of the product on the East Coast and Bacon knew that he would have to get Juan to load him up with a good supply if he was going to make the major moves the way he wanted.

Red and Bacon arrived in Cancún and headed toward their luxurious leased four-bedroom, three-bathroom private villa overlooking the water. Red quickly became accustomed to the special amenities: concierge services, a complimentary car and access to a private pool, several tennis courts and the putting greens. The villas also had their own spa and massage services.

Once they were inside, Red stood mesmerized at the sliding glass door at the back of the kitchen and gazed out over the water, enjoying the spectacular view of their getaway. The sun-dappled sea sparkled blue and serene. It looked magical.

Bacon watched Red as she stared out over the sea, then he walked up behind her. Wrapping his arms around her waist and pulling her into him, he spoke. "We're going to try that out when we get back."

"Sounds like a good idea," Red said, taking his hand. She led him to the front door and chirped. "Ooh Bacon, let's go to L'Chic! There's something—"

"Chill, ma," Bacon said, laughing at her excitement. "I have to meet with my boy Juan first."

"Aw, c'mon," Red protested. "We just got here and I haven't even been in a store yet. C'mon, Bacon." She whined like a spoiled little girl.

He shook his head humorously. "You'll have to wear something you already have," he told her. "You have a boutique in that walk-in closet in the master bedroom. And what's wrong with what you already have on?"

Red looked at him incredulously. "I wore this for the flight." She ran her hand down the pink, orange and yellow floral sundress, trying to straighten out imaginary wrinkles.

"It looks good on you, baby," Bacon said, pulling her close once again. "You're going to knock my man dead."

Bacon took Red to the docks, where a skiff was waiting to whisk them across the sun-spangled water to Juan's yacht. After a short jaunt across the gently rolling waves, they were escorted onboard by some of Juan's men. The yacht was a 300-foot Christensen, with five private staterooms, a gym, a theater, a swimming pool, a Jacuzzi and its own Jet Ski ramps and helicopter pad. Red figured that Juan had to be the numero uno head of a major organization to roll like this. She could smell money sweetening the air, and Red wondered if Juan had a taste for caramel chocolate. She could upgrade and get rid of Bacon's stank ass but that would mess up her plans for him. Perhaps she could see what Juan was about after she exacted her revenge on Bacon, she considered.

Bacon exchanged handshakes with a short, stout Latino man, and then turned toward her. "Juan, I want you to meet my lady, Raven."

Juan lifted Red's hand to his lips and kissed it gently. "A pleasure to meet you, *señorita*. I love to have beautiful women aboard my yacht."

"Thank you." Red smiled.

Bacon exchanged hugs with another gentleman on the boat, and then turned toward Red. "Red, this is my dude Blue. He handles things for me in New York."

Red was speechless. Her heart skipped several beats and her palms instantly became sweaty. She swallowed hard suddenly. She couldn't believe her eyes or her ears. Blue was actually standing before her, and he actually worked for Bacon. By now, her legs began to feel wobbly and she felt the need to sit down, and she definitely needed a drink. Summoning up every bit of willpower in her body, she had maintained her composure, and extended her hand, to him.

"A pleasure to meet you," Blue said, not tipping his hand, either.

Red wondered why Blue didn't let Bacon know that they knew each other. She wondered why he was holding his cards close to his chest as well. Blue was always up to something, so it couldn't be for any good reason. She would definitely have to be on her guard.

"Keep the lady company while Bacon and I go below and talk for little while," Juan told Blue. "My staff will get you anything you need." He looked at Red. "Are you hungry, *señorita*?"

Red shook her head. "Not right now, thank you."

"You let my man know what you want, and they will get it for you," Juan told her. "My chef is excellent. He'll prepare anything you like."

"Thank you." Red smiled.

Juan placed a hand on Bacon's shoulder and the two of them headed belowdecks. Red turned to Blue.

"What are you doing here?"

Blue smiled mischievously. "I work for Bacon."

"This is bullshit! Out of all the niggas you could work for, Blue. Why Bacon? Damn!" Red protested. "Does he know about us?"

Blue shook his head. "I ain't told him."

She eyed him evilly, then shook her head in disgust.

"So, where's Sasha?" Red asked, harshly. She still couldn't believe that he had hooked up with one of her girls.

"Sasha ain't my business no more."

"Oh really?" Red lifted an eyebrow. "Is that how you do it? Hit 'em and leave 'em?"

"You left me, remember?"

"And for good reason. Remember?" Red defended with her hands on her hips. "Did she leave your trifling ass, too?"

Blue waved his hand, dismissing the question. "Forget about her. I wanna know what's up with you."

"What about me?" she countered.

"I'm trying to see about you, Red," Blue said, licking his lips.

"You know, I ain't never had a problem spending big to get what I want."

Red nodded. That was true. Blue was the biggest trick east of the Mississippi. He bought pussy like an investor bought stocks.

"So what's up, Red? We gonna do Mexico together?"

"Blue, you can't handle me anymore," Red said tartly and walked off.

"That's what you think," Blue muttered, watching that fine, fine ass strut away from him.

CHAPTER TWENTY-FIVE

Q thought about what he had seen on the tape and was even more convinced that Red didn't intend to shoot him. It was hard to believe, but deep down, he knew that she couldn't have shot him on purpose. He was still upset that she hadn't been to the hospital to see him, though. Even though he still loved Red, he knew he had to let go emotionally.

"Hey, Quentin!" Chass chirped as she entered his room wearing a big smile. She hadn't forgotten how he spoke to her, but she wanted things to really work out for them, so she was willing to forgive him.

"Hi, Chass," he acknowledged, putting the tapes in his closet for safekeeping.

"What are you doing?" she asked him.

"Nothing, just trying to stay busy."

"I understand," she told him. "Hey, I went by your place and got some more clothes for you. I can take your old ones back home and wash them."

"Okay," he confirmed. "Hey look"—he turned and looked at Chass—"I'm sorry for the way I acted the other day. I'm just tired of being cooped up, that's it."

"I understand, Quentin. You don't have to apologize."

"Mr. Carter, are you ready?" the cute therapist asked as she came through the door.

He walked slowly over to his wheelchair and plopped down. She pushed him out of the room.

Chass looked around. *What was he really doing in that closet?* she asked herself. Since he was already down the hall, she walked to the closet and began to check through his things. She felt something hard, in a pocket, so she pulled it out. A videotape?

She turned around to make sure the coast was still clear, then stuffed the tapes into the dirty clothes that she was taking home to wash for him.

Chass's busy body plopped down on her couch after sticking the tape into her VCR. She was glad she hadn't gotten rid of the old machine. She would wash the clothes later, but she wanted to know what was on the tape first. Her mouth dropped when she saw Red suddenly appear. Disappointment spread across her face.

"Quentin's still in love with her," she said. "He's covering for her."

CHAPTER TWENTY-SIX

*T*he next day, Bacon opened the door to the villa to find Blue standing before him.

"Yo, what's happenin?" Bacon greeted him.

"You know what it is," Blue said, exchanging handshakes and giving Bacon a one-armed shoulder bump.

Bacon waved for him to come in. Once inside, Blue looked around, taking in the luxurious accommodations.

"Can I get you something?" Bacon asked, walking over to the wet bar. He poured himself a glass of Ciroc and pineapple juice.

"I'll have whatever you having."

Bacon poured another glass and handed it to Blue.

"So what brings you by? I don't have anything finalized yet," Bacon admitted, sitting down on the sofa. He picked up the remote and pressed "play." He wanted to finish watching the rest of *Scarface.* Slowly he sipped on his drink.

The two men sat and watched the rest of the gangster flick.

Once it was over, Blue asked, "Yo, where shorty at?" He had fin-ished his drink.

"She restin', man. She went out shopping earlier. You know how they do, spend up all yo' money before you can even make it, then come home bone tired."

They both laughed.

"Yo, Bacon," Blue said. "I can push two more kilos if you get-ting extra weight. I pretty much got the Bronx on lock and just secured my soldiers in Jersey. Got real niggas that hungry, man, and wanna eat."

Bacon looked at Blue. "You know, I like you. You ambi-tious."

"Shit, a nigga gotta do what he gotta do."

"That's right," Bacon acknowledged.

Just then, Bacon's cell phone rang. He slid the "talk" bar to the right and answered it. "Speak."

Blue looked toward the bedroom, wondering if Red was really sleeping.

Bacon got up off the couch.

On the other side of the door, Red was fuming. *What the fuck is that nigga doing here? That nigga just tried to ruin my shit with Bacon,* she whispered to herself in disbelief, *but why didn't he just tell him we fucked around? He making it seem like I'm this scandalous heifer, but he got everything he deserved.* She thought back to how Blue had played her when she was younger. She smiled when she remembered him eating the dooky-filled enchi-ladas at her crib.

Blue was playing his cards too close to his chest. Now she would have to sting him, too. She went to her drawer and grabbed her tiny digital recorder, then returned to the door and opened it a crack.

"Yo, I'ma take this call real quick," Bacon told Blue and stepped out onto the balcony.

Once Bacon was out of ear range, Blue pulled out his Black-Berry and dialed a number.

"Yo, what up? Yeah, I need to know about the deal on old girl's head, and if it's still good . . . Naw, what I'm saying is, I got old girl, and if the bounty is still in effect, I can get her." Blue confirmed. "Yeah, yeah." There was a momentary silence, then he spoke again. "Yeah, yeah, the other chick been taken care of back in New York. That was hard, though, man, 'cause she was carrying my seed. But this ho is more, right?"

Oh, my God, Red thought. *There was a bounty on Sasha's head* and *mine? Fuck!!!* She wanted to run out of the room and have Bacon kill Blue, but she had to get herself together.

Red paced back and forth nervously. She had to come up with something quick to handle Blue before he could handle her. She had an idea who was calling the shots behind the scenes, but she would have to confirm it first. Then she would have to come up with a plan to take care of them both.

"I'ma handle my business. I'll let you know exactly when and where," Blue said into his phone, then ended his call.

"Let me know when and where, you son of a bitch!" Red spat venomously, striding into the room.

"I knew your scandalous ass wasn't asleep," Blue told her as she walked out of the bedroom.

"So, you killed her, huh?"

"What are you talking about?" Blue smiled.

"You sorry, little-dick, shit-eating bastard!" Red snarled, then remembered Bacon was close by. She didn't want to alert him that something was wrong.

"Little dick, huh? You liked it."

"I liked your money, you stupid muthafucka. Why you have that girl killed?"

An exasperated laugh escaped Blue's lips. "You didn't give a fuck about Sasha," he told her, "and you know it. Let's just keep it real. You wanted to get her for fucking with me anyway."

"She didn't deserve to die!" Red countered.

"What's this?" Blue asked, raising his hands into the air. "Oh, so now since you fucking with Bacon, you a mighty baller's bitch and you got some type of conscience now? You ain't never had one before but you got one now? You fake, Red. You don't give a shit about anyone but yourself and you know that."

"You right, I didn't like her with you, but damn, you got that bitch pregnant and you still killed her? You a cold, heartless son of a bitch!"

"Like you give a fuck?" Blue jeered, throwing his hands up. "So what? I set the bitch up and I had her killed! So the fuck what? I fucked her over before you could. Is that why you mad, Red? Because I got to her first? You're just like me so don't stand there and pretend you're any different. You use people to get what you want, and then you throw them away like dirty towels. I used Sasha, and she served me, did whatever the fuck I said. She was a true ride-or-die chick, Red. Someone you could have taken lessons from. Yeah, she was carrying my seed, but like they say, Bounty is the quicker picker-upper, and in the end, money talks and bullshit walks. She got used for what she was good for."

"Using folks, huh?" Red repeated, then frowned. "Is that what you're doing to Bacon?"

"Why do you care?" Blue smiled. "You're using him to get the lifestyle you want, and so am I, so at the end of the day, we're both the same."

"And if I tell him?"

"Tell him what?" Blue said, stepping in her face. "How I used to fuck you? Do you really want to tell him that? Niggas like

Bacon don't want to hear that shit. You think a baller want to hear that his girl used to fuck with a nigga that works for him?"

Blue laughed. "You tell him that, and you'll be out on the streets like yesterday's trash. No, you ain't gonna tell him shit."

"You try anything, and I swear, Bacon will kill you," Red threatened. "I ain't no weak-ass bitch like Sasha."

An evil smile spread across Blue's face. "Tell your man that I had to step out, but I'll get with him later."

"Fuck you."

Blue stepped around Red and headed out the door. When he was gone, Red pulled her tiny digital recorder out of her pocket and played back the conversation that she had just recorded. Sure enough, the recorder had worked and recorded everything loud and clear. "I got you now, you son of a bitch." Blue had just confessed on tape to killing Sasha for money.

CHAPTER TWENTY-SEVEN

*D*etective Thomas pulled up to the house, parked his car, then walked up the driveway to the spacious home. Once he got to the front door, he spied the doorbell on the wall to the side of the door and pressed the button.

"Damn, who is it now?" Red cursed. She leaned forward and turned the shower handle to the off position. The steaming hot water immediately ceased to pour from the showerhead, and Red reached out of the shower stall for a thick towel. "Bacon, you better not have forgotten your key again."

The bell rang again.

"Coming!" Red shouted. After wrapping herself in the towel, she stepped out of the shower and headed for the front door.

She swung it open, only to find Detective Thomas standing before her. He took a good look at her long, curly red hair and her soft, glistening, toffee-colored skin with just a hint of red undertones—perfect. Her skin was perfect, not a pimple in sight.

A lump quickly formed in his throat. He hadn't known how beautiful she actually was until then.

"Raven Gomez?" Detective Thomas asked.

Red nodded. "Yeah, it's me."

"I'm Detective Thomas from the Detroit Police Department. May I come in?"

Reluctantly, and trying not to hide her nervousness, Red nodded and stepped to the side. "Come in."

Detective Thomas stepped inside Bacon's house and looked around. He noted the luxurious furnishings, the high-dollar electronics and the sheer opulence of the home.

He whistled. "Wow! Nice place."

"Thank you," Red said with a slight edge to her voice. For the first time, she wondered about the wisdom of letting a police officer inside her home. After all, Bacon wasn't exactly an upstanding citizen with a legit job. He was a dope dealer, with a high-dollar crib and custom-made furniture. Allowing the detective inside to inspect things could invite the narcotics division into their lives, and if Bacon came home while Thomas was still there, Red didn't want to think of what would happen. Detective Thomas was a distraction that she didn't need right now. He could cause more problems than he was worth.

"You live here alone?"

"No, it's actually my boyfriend's place."

"Lucky you," Detective Thomas said with a smile. "What is he, a professional athlete?"

"Business owner."

"Really?" The detective lifted an eyebrow. "Of what? Anything I've heard of?"

Red shrugged. "What can I do for you today, Detective?"

Detective Thomas smiled. "You're a hard one to find."

"Why is that? My driver's license is registered to this address."

"May I?" Thomas asked, waving his hand toward a spot on the couch.

Red exhaled. "Suit yourself."

She could tell that he wasn't going to be that easy to get rid of. Good thing for her that Bacon was going to be gone for a while. Still, having a homicide detective inside her home sniffing around wasn't a good thing. She would have to be on her toes.

Detective Thomas seated himself on the couch. "I was wondering if I could ask you a few more questions about Ezekiel Morrison?"

Red rolled her eyes.

"Don't worry, this is just an interview. You're not in any trouble or under arrest or anything. I just have a few simple questions."

"Go ahead," Red told him. She knew she had a right to be worried. He was snooping around about that bastard Zeke. The good thing was that he wasn't here to arrest her. At least not yet, but still, she had this stupid shit hanging over her head, as well as that shit with Q. She had to get rid of some of this shit off her back. She was putting her plan in place to get even with everyone, and she certainly didn't need the police on her back. Actually, she needed to get them on her side.

Thomas pulled out his notepad.

"One thing," Red told him.

"What's that?"

"I'm kinda in a hurry, so you're going to have to ask me what you need to ask while I get dressed. Is that okay?"

Thomas shrugged. "Sure, I don't mind."

"Cool." Red turned, walked into the bathroom and gathered her hairbrush, some coconut oil and her underwear. She dried herself off, slipped into her bra and panties, wrapped a dry towel back around her body and returned to the living room with the rest of her materials.

She stood just in front of the detective and rested her petite foot on the coffee table, then began to pour the coconut oil into her hand. After rubbing her hands together she bent over and slowly rubbed the oil up and down her leg. Thomas watched as her shapely, long, taut, sinewy leg turned a silky, smooth, coppery red as the oil soaked into her pores. The observant detective noticed that her feet were small, and her toenails were perfectly manicured with French tips. He loved pretty feet. A woman who took care of her feet was a definite turn-on for him. Most women took care of fingernails and the parts of the body that everyone could see—their hair, their face—but the ones who took care of the parts that weren't too visible every day were perfect in his mind. Again, a lump formed in his throat.

Red watched his reaction to what she was doing. His eyes were following her hands as they glided up and down her legs. He looked like a hungry dog eyeing a thick T-bone steak, ready to devour if just given the chance. She knew that she had him.

Red had a trump card to play, and it was the one card that she had always played. It was the one card that she had played her entire life. Her body. She would use her body as her defense. It was her one weapon, and she was a master at using it.

Men had wanted her as far back as she could remember. Her good looks, coupled with her sexy body, made men accept the unacceptable, forget the unforgettable and believe the unbelievable. She planned on using what God blessed her with to see if she could make this detective believe her. Make him her friend. She would see if she could make him be her defender in a world that was slowly closing in on her.

Red continued to slowly rub the oil all over her legs and arms, massaging them in a seductive manner, and then she looked at the detective.

"You don't mind, do you?" she asked innocently, grabbing at her towel.

Thomas shook his head and swallowed hard. He could barely speak. "No, go ahead." He was enjoying the show.

She dropped her towel, and began to add more oil to her body. Detective Thomas observed that not only did she have no fat, but also she had rock-hard abs and a firmly toned body all around. She had no blemishes, no cuts, no scars, no nothing. Her svelte body was perfect.

"This is what I hate the most," Red told him with a slight smile.

"What is that?" Thomas asked. He was having difficulties concentrating on what brought him to the mansion because his manhood was growing by the second and as if it were about to snap in two. He began to fidget on the sofa, trying to get more comfortable.

"I can't reach my back," Red complained. "Who wants a dry itchy back all day? Would you?"

"Would I what?" Thomas asked.

"Hook a sister up?" Red asked, handing him the oil.

Detective Thomas stood slowly, shifting his dick in his pants. It still stuck out, revealing that he was rock hard. He wanted some of Red badly. Thomas took the oil, squeezed some onto his hand and then rubbed it onto Red's back. He was just about at his breaking point. Red knew by his trembling hands that she had him. She also looked down out of the corner of her eye, and noticed his hard-on saluting her.

"How long have you known Ezekiel?" Thomas asked, trying to remember what brought him here.

Red shrugged. "Since I've been knowing Q. They were partners."

Detective Thomas walked his eyes up and down her body and swallowed hard. "Were you two close?"

Red shook her head. "Not at all."

"Were you friends?"

"We knew of each other."

"So you weren't buddies or anything."

"Not in the least."

Thomas eyeballed her ass, scarcely covered by her barely legal panties. "You were there at the apartment the day he died?" Somehow he managed to get this thought together to question her.

Red nodded.

The detective's voice broke. "I'm done."

"Thanks," she told him, taking the oil from his hand. "I'm really in a hurry."

"Well, then I'll get out of your way," Thomas told her. "I can see that you're busy."

Red walked Thomas to the door. "I still have your card, Detective."

Thomas nodded. "Use it, any time you need anything."

Red opened the door for the detective and smiled at him. "I will."

"You have a good day," Thomas told her.

"You, too," Red replied softly. She closed the door. She wanted desperately to laugh, but didn't out of fear that he might hear her. She had him, and she knew it. She had just gone through an interview without the detective asking her one single fucking question of any substance. Thomas would fit right into her little plan of revenge. Tonight, she was going to celebrate with Bacon, get him drunk at the club and then complete the next step in her plan.

CHAPTER TWENTY-EIGHT

*T*hat evening, Bacon stumbled forward, still holding his bottle of Grey Goose. It was an $80 bottle of imported French vodka, his favorite, and he was determined not to drop it.

"Open the door, baby!" he slurred.

Red locked the door of the black Range Rover and rushed to Bacon. She interlocked her arm with his to keep him from stumbling.

"Red, that's what I'm talking about!" Bacon shouted. "You got my back, baby."

"I always got your back," she assured him as she struggled to lead him to the door. "Hold on, just try to stand up straight."

"I can't believe my nigga is gone," Bacon said solemnly.

Tonight's festivities had been twofold. One, they were celebrating the money that Bacon had been raking in since his new deal with his Mexican connection. He had basically taken over the streets in Detroit, and was pushing his product in Flint, Saginaw and Lansing, and even had Blue pushing his product well into New York and New Jersey. For the first time the product was moving from Detroit to New York, instead of the other way around. This had made Bacon very rich. In fact, he had so much money that he didn't know what to do with it all. He had started opening up Laundromats, beauty salons and barbershops, car dealerships and nightclubs. The money was flowing too fast to keep up with.

The second reason for the night's festivities was to toast Bacon's homeboy, Mike, who was recently killed by carjackers while rolling down the streets of Philly in his Bentley. The ballers in Detroit were up in arms and heated about their homeboy's death. They had all gathered to toast him and give him a proper farewell, since his funeral would be held in North Carolina where he grew up as a child, and where his parents now lived once again.

"Hurry up, girl!" Bacon slurred.

Red fumbled with her key and finally got it into the lock. She opened the door and helped Bacon inside. He stumbled and somehow managed to land on the couch.

"Damn, you're heavy!" Red fussed, huffing and puffing.

"That's from good eatin', Red!" Bacon laughed an alcoholic laugh. He slapped his stomach. "That's them steaks, girl!"

"Baby, I'ma run you a hot shower."

Bacon clasped her hand and pulled her down onto him. "I don't want no shower! I want some of you."

"Boy, you need a shower."

"Shower me with your love," Bacon began singing.

Red burst into laughter. "You are fucked up."

Bacon looked over at his coffee table. Stacks were piled onto the table, twenties and hundreds, covering the entire top. An electronic money counter also sat on the table.

"Watch this shit, Red." Bacon smiled. He took a stack of loose bills, placed them in the money counter and watched the machine go to work flipping the bills. "I love that shit!"

Again, Red laughed. "You're crazy."

"What we gonna do with all this shit, Red?"

Red shrugged. She had already begun stealing stacks of money from Bacon. Once he couldn't count the money anymore, he stopped being careful, stopped caring about every penny. Red was more than happy to relieve him of some of it. After all he owed her.

"We're going to invest it, baby," Red told him. She dropped down beside him and pulled off his shoes.

Bacon stroked Red's hair. He was in seventh heaven. Red had done a one-eighty. She had changed completely, and she was now being wifey. She wasn't running the streets no more, she wasn't tripping with him about hitting the streets to handle his business, she was always where she said she was going to be and she was even trying to cook and clean and iron his clothes for him now. He had a beautiful, down-ass woman who took care of him. She was a baller's dream wife.

"I'm fucked up, ain't I?" Bacon hiccupped.

Red nodded. She helped him out of his shirt, and then out of his pants. "Come on, let's get you into bed."

"You take care of me, Red," Bacon slurred. "I'm always going to take care of you."

Red stopped and looked at him. Within seconds, her eyes became teary and her eyebrows crinkled. She began sobbing profusely.

"What's wrong?" Bacon asked.

"How, Bacon?" Red asked through fake tears. "How are you going to take care of me?"

"What do you mean?"

"Look at Mike. He was on top of his game and now he's dead.

What about his girlfriend? His kids? What they got now? They ain't got shit. If something happens to you, then what? What's going to happen to me then?"

"You get the money, Red," Bacon slurred. He picked up a pile of money from the table.

"How long is this shit gonna last?"

"This ain't all of what I got, girl. I'll tell you where the rest of it is," Bacon slurred. "You can have it. You can have it all."

"I can have it all so the police can come and arrest me and take it all?" Red cried. "We need some legitimate shit, Bacon, and life insurance. We can't keep living like this."

"We got businesses." Bacon laughed.

"What's so funny?" As if on cue, Red started crying heavily. "See, that's what I'm talking about. You don't take me seriously."

Bacon caressed her head. "I do, baby. If that's what you want we can go get some tomorrow."

"These people sent me the papers," Red told him. "I can mail it off tomorrow, and we'll be taken care of."

Red rose and pulled some papers out of her purse. She handed them to Bacon, along with a pen. She started crying again.

"Shhhhh," Bacon said, caressing her head.

"I just want to do something for us." Red told him through sniffles.

"Where do I sign them?" Bacon asked without even bothering to read the documents.

Red pointed at the places Bacon need to sign, and he took the pen and put his John Hancock on them where she told him to. He barely made it through before leaning back and passing out.

Red gathered the papers and carefully placed them in her purse. A gigantic smile spread across her face. She had just gotten Bacon to sign a quitclaim deed giving her back her real estate company, and the closing documents for the sale of the house.

"Checkmate, muthafucka!" Red spat, standing over a snoring conked-out Bacon. She had just taken a giant leap in her plan to fuck over those who had fucked her over.

CHAPTER TWENTY-NINE

Red sat in the chair while Donna dried her hair. Donna was her latest stylist at the Divas salon, a new shop Red had been trying out on the north side of town, and she was loving it. She had been going to Donna for three weeks now, and girlfriend was all that she was cracked up to be. Donna was a stylist who was in the game along with her man, so naturally, all of the big ballers' wives and wifeys went to her. She was the "in" stylist of the moment.

Donna was a Dominican who had moved to Detroit from New York. She was top flight when it came to doing hair. She was the baddest thing east of LA when it came to cuts and styling. She was also bad with a weave, especially infusions and quick weaves.

"What you think? Is it time?" Red asked.

"Time for what?" Donna replied.

"Time to take it all off?"

"Bitch, please!" Donna told her. "I ain't cutting your hair, or letting anybody else do it. You gonna have to whip my ass if you want all of this pretty red hair cut off."

Red laughed. She wasn't chopping off her hair for nobody. She just liked to tease Donna.

The door to the shop flew open and in walked a tall chocolate female with a pixie cut. "Stop, drop and roll, bitches! Fire is in the house!"

All of the beauticians in the shop broke into laughter.

"Foxy, shut your ass up!" Donna told her.

"Ms. Foxy is here for her weekly do." She walked up to a display cabinet and eyed the beauty products for sale. "I need me a perm, and some spikes, and some highlights. I'm trying to get ten more bitches hating on me by sundown."

"Bitch, you next," Ciara told her.

Foxy walked to the waiting area, picked up a hair magazine, took a seat and started flipping through the pages. "I need to pick me out a style that will make all of the bitches just go ahead and put that gun to they head and say forget it, they can't catch me."

Donna laughed. "That bitch is crazy."

Red looked over at the waiting area. She didn't recognize Foxy, but knew there was something strange about her. Foxy was a post-op transvestite, with breasts, a quick weave and all of the features to match. Her jaw was a little too square, and her Adam's apple a little too visible not to be noticed. And despite how she had changed her voice, she still sounded like a teenage boy trying to be a diva. Her expensive hormone shots helped get rid of the bass, softened her up a lot and did wonders in getting rid of all the hair, but they still couldn't put her all of the way over the hump.

"Girl, is that a man?" Red asked quietly.

Donna bumped Red. "Girl, stop."

"Is it?"

"She used to be," Donna whispered. "She had it snipped and tucked."

"No!" Red giggled under her breath.

"Girl, what are you reading?" Foxy shouted across the room.

One of the beauty shop's customers was reading *Bitch Nigga, Snitch Nigga*.

"You don't know nothing about that book!" Ciara told Foxy.

"I know everything about it!" Foxy said, snapping her fingers. "From the Catfish to the Bacon, to all the food groups, girl!"

Everyone in the shop laughed.

"I can tell you about Ms. Lennox, and the whole nine yards!"

"Girl, you know Foxy is like dialing 411 in the hood!" Donna shouted.

Red sat up a little. *Who is this punk?*

"I can tell you who shot who, who snitched on who and who is still doing who and what," Foxy continued. "Hell, that story is so crazy and it is still going on. Shit, now the nephews is all involved. Niggas is still shooting niggas over bitches, bitches faking babies and blaming it on other niggas. Niggas putting out hits on other niggas, and bitches getting killed. Girl, it ain't over. They gonna kill that nigga who wrote the book, the bitch that stole the book and everyone in between."

Red went stiff. This punk was running his mouth and telling everything—shit that most motherfuckers didn't know and didn't need to know, but what did she know about the nephews? What did she know about bitches faking babies, and niggas shooting each other over bitches? *This whore knows too much*, Red thought. But even worse, he was telling too much.

"Girl, how do you know?" Ciara asked.

"'Cuz I do." Foxy laughed. "Hell, niggas talk like bitches do."

"Yeah, they do!" one of the shop's patrons chimed in.

"Amen, I second that!" Donna cackled.

"Especially when it comes to pillow talk." Foxy laughed

again. "Give a nigga some poohnanny and they can't shut the fuck up!"

The ladies in the shop howled with laughter.

"FBI be trying to bust a nigga and get 'em to snitch," Ciara added. "All they need to do is give them niggas some pussy. They'll learn where all the dope is!"

Again, laughter and howls shot throughout the shop.

"Especially this poohnanny," Foxy said, touching her hip with her index finger. "I give my little slice of bacon some of this, and he can't shut the fuck up."

Red gasped.

She was seated in the last chair in the shop, far enough away so that Foxy wasn't paying her any attention. The shop was narrow, but extremely long, placing Red a good distance away from the waiting area but still within hearing distance. Besides, she had a cape covering her clothing and a towel still wrapped around her wet hair. Red was a well-known female, and if this Foxy was fucking with Bacon, then she would know her. She had to keep a low profile and just listen.

As Red's ears burned it all started making sense. *So Bacon has been spilling the beans to Foxy, and somehow things have gotten back to Q. Which means that Foxy knows Q, or somebody Foxy ran her mouth to knows Q, and maybe even Bacon, too.* One thing was for certain: Red knew that she had discovered a major flow of information. It was this punk-ass tranny who had thrown some monkey wrenches in her game. Ms. Foxy was now on her list, and would have to be dealt with.

"Girl, relax," Donna told her. "You're tenser than a piece of steel right now."

Red exhaled, and tried to relax in the chair. "Stress."

"Well, don't let it make your hair come out," Donna told her. "You do anything to mess up this pretty hair, and me and you gon' have some problems."

"I won't."

"So how you want it today?"

"Girl, just blow-dry it, and put a flat iron to it so it'll have some body to it."

"You got it," Donna told her.

Yeah, Red thought, *I got it and then some.* That filthy fucking Bacon was running up in a tranny *and* fucking her. Either being in prison had really fucked him up, or he was a sick son of a bitch from the get-go. Whatever it was, he and his little tranny girlfriend were gonna get it.

CHAPTER THIRTY

*C*atfish made his way through the inmate side of the visiting room, cursing the entire time. He had to rush and get dressed. His khaki uniform was wrinkled from not being ironed because he hadn't been expecting a visitor. He hadn't had his hair braided, nor had he had time to shave in anticipation of his visit. Everything had come as a complete surprise to him.

He wondered who it could be visiting him today. His mother hadn't told him that she was coming, and she and his sister were the only people who still visited him. His girl was long gone, and so were his homies. Sure he had loyal soldiers who were still on the payroll, but they certainly hadn't made the trek upstate to pay him a visit today.

"Booth number five!" the guard told him.

Catfish shuffled down the corridor until he found the booth. He was shocked to see who was sitting and waiting for him.

"What the fuck are you doing here?" Catfish demanded.

"Sit down," Red said calmly.

"I ought to snap your damn neck!" he hissed.

"Sit your ass down and listen to me," Red told him.

"For what?" Catfish looked around the room. He stared at the guard near the exit and thought about walking out of the visiting room. He had nothing to say to Red. She had screwed him and he wanted her dead.

"Because it costs you nothing to hear me out. What else you gotta do? Go back to your cell and jack off?"

"That's better than sitting here listening to your bullshit," Catfish barked. "Don't you realize that I can still reach out and touch you?"

Red nodded. "I know that, but we can fuck over each other."

"You got a lot of nerve coming here!" he snapped.

"Sit down, and let's talk business. We can both win."

"You're a snitch, Red—or should I call you Lisa?"

"You and I both know I didn't write that book."

"You making money off of real niggas' backs."

"And now you should make some money, too."

Catfish paused and stared at her. "What are you talking about?"

"It's your story, you're a part of it, you should get paid, too."

He pulled the seat out from the desk on his side of the booth and sat down. "You better come correct because I can kill you right here and right now. If I feel like I'm being played, I'll reach across this booth on your ass and it's nothing anyone can do to stop me."

"If you feel like that, then you can walk away."

"No, I'ma snap your damn neck!"

"Okay, then snap my neck." Red remained calm. "I got a money-making proposal for you. You want to make money or not?"

Catfish quieted his ranting. "Let's hear it."

"I hear they got a lot of talent in the joint."

Catfish pursed his lips and nodded slowly.

Goddamn, you ugly, Red thought. His narrow face, bugged-out eyes and scraggly mustache made him look just like a catfish—a bottom feeder.

"You know any good writers in there?" Red asked.

Catfish smiled slightly. He automatically knew where she was going. "I know a couple of cats in here who can write."

Red shrugged. "They want a part two, and I damn sure can't write it."

"What are we talking?" Catfish asked.

"We split the advance down the middle."

"How much?"

"Fifty grand."

Catfish shook his head. "I need more than that."

"Look, I'm handling all the paperwork, the marketing, the book signings, all of the travel and bullshit."

"Yeah, but without me, there ain't no book."

"Says who?" Red smiled. "I came to you to give you first shot at making some bread. I'm sure I can find a nigga in the joint who read *Snitch Nigga, Bitch Nigga* and who's willing to contribute his talent."

"Then why did you come to me?" Catfish asked. He leaned back in his seat.

"'Cause I want a full partnership."

"A partnership with you, Red? That's asking for trouble."

"How? You can reach out and touch me from the joint, remember?"

"No, you remember that."

"Look, I want to call it quits between us."

"What do you mean?" Catfish frowned.

"We become partners, you call off the hit—take the price off of my head—and we make money on this book thing," Red told him. "You know the story, the players, the real deal of what happened behind the scenes. You tell the story and get somebody to do a banging part two, and I handle shit out here on the streets, and we make money together."

"Why should I do it? What makes you think that I need any money?"

"We'll go fifty-fifty on the royalties, too," Red told him.

Catfish raised an eyebrow. Everybody knew that *Snitch Nigga, Bitch Nigga* had been a bestseller and had made a killing. Getting in on that and refreshing his bank would be real nice, Catfish thought. But still, he didn't know about getting into business with Dirty Red.

"What about Bacon?" Catfish asked.

"What about him?"

"Why should I create unnecessary beef with that man?"

"Won't be no beef," Red told him. "I'm Lisa Lennox, remember? This is my shit now. Bacon letting me run this."

"Did he send you here?"

Red shook her head. "Of course not."

"Why he ain't write part two?" Catfish asked.

"'Cause he don't give a fuck about no writing no more," Red explained. "He did that shit while he was locked down. Now that he out, he too busy hustling."

Catfish nodded. He had heard that Bacon was the man on the street now. "I don't know, Red. It sounds suspicious to me. Like a setup, but I can't put my finger on it. I don't know what angle you coming from, or what you plan on doing, 'cause you a scandalous bitch, but if you think that I'm gonna have somebody write a book, and then you not give me my half, you're sadly mistaken. I'll fuck you faster than you can fart."

Red nodded.

"Sasha fucked me over, and you see where she at?" Catfish told her. "I'll have you done just like I had that bitch done. You got me, Red?"

Red nodded again and extended her hand. Catfish shook it.

"Call off the bounty," Red told him.

Catfish agreed. "You just remember your little friend, and what happened to her," he repeated.

Red rose from her seat. "Nice seeing you."

She definitely would remember Sasha and what that bastard had done to her. Now she had her evidence, and she also had a new detective friend to put everything into place. She just needed to make a few more moves, and then she would get Catfish to do what she needed him to do; after that she'd take care of his ass.

"Next time give me some notice," Catfish told her.

Red walked out of the visiting room and headed for the prison exit. She had gotten out of there just in time. The tiny recorder she had hidden in her bra was pinching her breasts.

"I got your ass too, you bitch nigga, snitch nigga," Red said to herself. She was going to fry Catfish's ass to protect herself, and to get revenge for Sasha. Now that he would call off the hit, she had bought herself some time to finish taking care of her other business. Now it was a race to get Catfish before he could get her.

Red walked through the parking lot with a sinister grin on her face. Everything was almost in place. She just needed to move one more major piece on the board and that was to get Detective Thomas completely on her side.

CHAPTER THIRTY-ONE

*Y*o, baby, can I get those digits?"

Laquisha Denny waved the stranger off as she climbed out of her straight-from-the-showroom-floor, Obsidian black BMW 760 Li sedan. Being a sinewy, six-foot, 140-pound, copper-skinned beauty, she was used to strangers trying to get her number. Catcalls, whistles, shouts; nothing fazed her anymore. She was beautiful, and she knew it. Family, friends and strangers, everyone had told her that her entire life. In fact it had reached the point that she now considered it a nuisance when someone tried to holler at her. She had a man anyway. A good man. Her brand-new $100,000-plus BMW was proof of that.

Treagen had provided for her well. He was a straight hustler, in every sense of the word. He had been a baller since the age of sixteen, having bought his first bird at the age of fifteen. The streets had consumed him from the age of twelve. From there powder became crack, and rocks became packs, and packs became quarters; and eventually he worked his way up to ounces.

Trap had set up trap houses in almost every project in the Motor City. He had them organized with lookers out front and cashiers to take the customer's money and a separate house where the merchandise was picked up. He had everyone communicating by cheap walkie-talkies that he purchased from Radio Shack. Setting up trap houses was how he made his big break, his reputation and his name. He went from being Treagen, to Lil' Trap, to just Trap in a matter of three years. It was during this time that he first met Laquisha.

Laquisha had always been the good girl in school. She was the spoiled little Ms. Perfect that all the dudes wanted to holler at, but were scared to. Trap didn't muster up the nerve to holler until after he had started balling and could hide behind his clothes, jewelry and cars. But once he did step to her, he found that she had been peeping at him for years. Their elementary school crush had blossomed into a high school love and spawned a forever love. She was his woman, and he was her man, and neither one of them could envision life without the other.

Laquisha closed the door to her Beemer and scanned around the parking lot. Trap had taught her to be aware of her environment. She wore too much expensive jewelry not to pay attention to her surroundings. Detroit was a hardscrabble town, with people always on the lookout for a quick come-up. Between her earrings, tennis bracelet, Piaget watch and the rings on her petite, manicured fingers, she was wearing a good hundred grand. And a hundred grand lick was too good for most people to pass up.

Today Laquisha was headed into the city for a hair appointment. She'd heard about a hot new stylist at a hot new shop called Divas, and she wanted to check things out for herself. Her usual stylist was out of town on vacation, so she decided it would be the perfect time to cheat on her and check out a new beautician. That's why she called and set an appointment with Donna, the red-hot Dominican from New York, to see what all the fuss was about.

Laquisha ran her hands over the legs of her crème-colored Ferragamo pantsuit, and double-timed it across the street to the shop. She was already impressed with the establishment. The parking lot was filled with all high-end vehicles, from Navigators to Beemers. There was even a Bentley and a Maserati parked near the front. This told her that the clientele was high-dollar, and high-dollar clientele didn't put up with bullshit. One little chemical burn, or slip of that curling iron, and all of your customers were gone.

Laquisha stepped inside, signed in and scanned the shop. A small waiting area was just off to the right. She took a seat and searched the coffee table for a current magazine.

Immediately Red's antennae went up. They said game recognized game—well, beauty recognized another beauty that day.

"Girl, your hair looks like you just got it done!" Red told her, making small talk.

"This mess?" Laquisha asked, lifting a strand of her hair. "Girl, I got this done last week."

"It's still cute."

"Thank you." Laquisha smiled. "And you talking about me? What about you? You working that hairstyle."

"Who did your hair? That feathered bob looks really good on you. It accentuates the shape of your face."

"Thank you," Laquisha repeated. She extended her hand. "My name is Laquisha. Everybody just calls me Quisha."

"Raven," Red said, shaking her hand. "But everybody calls me Red."

Laquisha laughed and nodded. "That name fits you. Your reddish-bronze skin, your reddish-bronze hair and you even have this reddish glow about you."

"Like the devil?" Red joked.

"No, girl, like a fiery personality. I'll bet you're feisty just like me."

Red nodded. "You bet your ass I am."

Laquisha smiled and turned toward the row of stylists. "So what's up with Ms. Donna?"

"Is that who you're here to see?"

Laquisha nodded.

Red leaned back and adjusted herself in her seat. "Girl, she is the bomb! The best stylist in Motown!"

"Did she do your hair?"

Red ran her fingers through her hair. "I've been coming to her for a few weeks now. And she got my shit soft, silky and looking good!"

"I see!"

"Your first time here?"

"Yep. I been going to this girl name Penny. She's been doing it for a while but I'm ready to try something different."

"Different? Like what?"

"I think I want a Mohawk. You seen Monica's hair on the BET Awards?"

"Ohhh, Monica was looking so fly!" Red snapped her fingers in the air. "I was like, go Monica, you looking good, girl!"

"I want something like that, but more of a Mohawk, and I want some blond in mines."

"Oh, I bet that would look so pretty on you."

"Thank you. I think it'll look good, too. I can go out and get my club on!"

"Hey!" Red said, laughing. "I ain't been clubbing in so long."

"Oh, girl, there's this new bar, it's called Bar Eleven. Have you heard of it?"

Red shook her head. "No, I haven't. How is it?"

"It is nice, with a nice atmosphere. It's a mixed crowd, and it's a twenty-five and older crowd, so ain't no kids up in there. They have an upstairs VIP section where you can look down on the dance floor."

"That sounds cool. I'ma have to go and check it out."

Laquisha pulled out her BlackBerry. "Girl, I'ma take you out and we're gonna party."

Red gave Laquisha her number. "My man is probably gonna want to go."

Laquisha shrugged. "Bring him. I'll bring Trap and we can introduce them."

"Well girl, Bacon is a little rough around the edges." Red laughed. "Be forewarned."

Laquisha laughed and waved her off. "Don't trip. Trap is the same way.

"Bacon . . . well, he's . . ."

"I already know what the deal is. Girl, my man is the same exact way. He's in the game, and judging by the shit you flossin', your man is, too. I already know. I ain't judging. Trap takes care of this. That black BMW outside is what he got Mama rolling in."

Red laughed. She felt relieved. She felt like she could relax and be herself around her new friend. Laquisha seemed like a real bitch and they had so much in common. She was down to earth, and she had found her a baller to take care of her. Hell, she wouldn't be surprised if Laquisha was from the projects just like she was.

"Girl, that black Range Rover is mines."

"See, Bacon takes care of his, just like Trap takes care of his. Girl, don't be embarrassed or ashamed. We ain't got nothing to apologize for or be ashamed of. Many bitches wish that they could be in our shoes."

"And look this good!" Red added.

"Amen!"

CHAPTER THIRTY-TWO

*B*ar Eleven was the Motor City's newest hot spot. It was the type of establishment that attracted a nice mixed crowd. The atmosphere was yuppie, with a little bit of grad school and old school thrown into the mix. It had a nice mid-twenties to mid-thirties crowd, with a few early-forties patrons thrown in for good measure. It was definitely not a place that attracted dope boys and ballers and it was the perfect place for Bacon and Red to get away from it all.

The bar was nestled inside an old two-story redbrick building near the city. The building had been an old factory of sorts, and the owner had renovated it thoroughly and installed a $30,000 sound system. The seating was burgundy leather sectionals arranged in seating groups, with small four-person tables and high chairs scattered throughout. The bar was against the far left side of the room, and a nice-size stage sat in the back of the bar for when they had poetry slam nights. The dance floor was in the center of the bar, and upstairs was the VIP section.

"I love this place!" Red shouted over the sound system.

"This is nice," Bacon concurred.

Red rushed to where Laquisha was standing and hugged her. Bacon followed close behind.

"Bacon, I want you to meet my girlfriend Laquisha," Red said, introducing them. "Quisha, this is Bacon."

Laquisha and Bacon exchanged handshakes, then Laquisha turned toward her guy. "This is my man Trap."

Trap and Red exchanged handshakes, followed by the two men shaking hands and hugging. The four of them gathered around one of the tall four-person pub tables scattered throughout. Even though there were seats available, the four of them remained standing. Red was hyped.

"This is the shit!" Red said excitedly. "I love the atmosphere and the music . . . that DJ has been jamming since we walked up in here."

"Girl, this is my song!" Laquisha lifted her hand and grooved to Guy's "Piece of My Love."

Red eyeballed Trap. He reminded her of Treach from Naughty by Nature. Not the Treach with the long braids, but the muscular, chocolate, bald-headed Treach with all the tats. Trap had a dangerous roughneck look about him but it was combined with the look of a sexy chocolate-skinned model. His Ed Hardy polo shirt and jeans made him look like a thug whose girl made him dress up. The two-inch-thick, diamond-filled platinum bracelet and diamond bezel Patek Philippe on his wrist and the long, thick platinum chain around his neck revealed his baller status. He looked like he came up hard on the streets and would kill a nigga in a heartbeat. He was a real dope boy and gangsta. Even though he belonged to her girl, Trap still made Red's pussy wet. All fine-ass ballers had that effect on her.

"So what up, my dude?" Bacon asked.

"Man, you know how it is," Trap answered. "Just creeping and crawling and trying not to get noticed."

"I hear you!" Bacon laughed. "Keep Uncle Johnny off ya ass."

"Shit!" Trap rubbed his face. "They out to get a nigga, huh?"

"It's all good, though. They got they role to play, we got ours."

"Damn straight."

"We just gotta keep it gangsta," Bacon told him. "These niggas out here gotta stop snitching."

"Man, I'ma buy you a drink on that one!" Trap laughed. He turned and headed for the bar.

"Cool people, Red!" Bacon laughed and nudged Red.

"Girl, you working that Mohawk!" Red exclaimed, examining Laquisha's hair.

"I wanted her to shave my hair shorter in the back though."

"Why? It looks good."

Bacon took in Laquisha. He liked them tall and slender, and Laquisha was just that, except for her ass. It had a ridiculous shape, Bacon thought. She had the kind of shape that niggas only dream about. She had an ass that you could sit a glass on top of, and virtually no stomach. It looked like she was carrying two pumpkins in her back pockets. Bacon smiled at the thought of getting a shot of Laquisha. He definitely wanted some of that.

Trap came back to the table with two drinks. He was followed by the barmaid, who was carrying two more. She set the drinks down and quickly disappeared. Trap handed Bacon his drink, and then raised his own in a toast.

"To new friends, and no snitches."

Red, Bacon and Laquisha lifted their drinks.

"No snitches," Bacon said. "Man, me and you are gonna have to get together."

Trap nodded. "No doubt, no doubt."

"Come to the club and we gonna kick it."

"What club is that?"

"I just opened up a new club called Club 313," Bacon said.

"No shit?" Laquisha asked. "I heard about that club. We been saying that we were going to go and check that place out."

"Oh, it's banging, baby!" Bacon bragged. He had opened it to help him wash some of his dope money, but the club turned out to be a phenomenal moneymaker itself. He didn't know what to do with all the money he was making, legal and illegal. Red was overjoyed.

"I'ma stop by there," Trap told him.

"Come by on Wednesday and let's talk some business."

"Okay, no business talk tonight." Red smiled. "We're here to have a good time."

"Let's dance, girl!" Laquisha grabbed Red's hand and the two of them trotted off to the dance floor. The DJ was bumping Jamie Foxx. "Girl, that's my song!"

Treagen nodded at Bacon's offer. He realized that Bacon was higher up on the food chain than he was, and that he was about to get put on. Maybe fucking with Bacon would be his way to come up and finally jump out of the game, he thought. He had some ideas that he wanted to push, and all he needed was a partner to get behind him. *Maybe Bacon is the one,* he thought.

CHAPTER THIRTY-THREE

*C*lub 313 occupied an entire building by itself. The building was enormous, as it had been a former Walmart. The discount chain had abandoned the building and built a glitzier, even more enormous building down the road, calling it a Super Walmart. No one in the city had use for the old building. It was too big for most other businesses to use. Bacon had come up with the idea of creating a super club inside.

Because the building had been abandoned for so long, Bacon had been able to get it for little more than a song and a dance. He poured massive amounts of money into it, in order to transform it into one of the largest clubs in the Midwest. The club had a $200,000 sound system, four dance floors, two massive bars, a 3,000-square-foot VIP section with its own bar, a game room filled with pool tables, a restaurant and even a small gift shop so that patrons could purchase shirts, caps, mugs and other club memorabilia. Bacon had created a first-class clubbing experience.

The first thing Trap noticed while walking up to the front door was the massive red neon sign on top of the club. The cursive script could be seen for miles. The club's front boasted dark tinted glass so the patrons couldn't be seen inside, and a rope guided the quickly forming line of partygoers inside. Several well-dressed security guards were standing outside keeping things orderly. Trap walked to the front of the line.

"May I help you, sir?" one of the guards asked.

"I'm on the VIP list," Trap replied.

"Name please?"

"Treagen . . . Trap, I mean. The name is Trap."

The guard checked the list he held in his hand, and then waved Trap through. It was crazy, Trap thought, stepping inside. The club wasn't even full yet, and still there was a line. The first thing that hit him inside was the décor, which was extremely modern, with lots of glass, chrome and LED lighting. The system also grabbed his attention. It was almost deafening.

"What up, my dude?" Bacon shouted.

"Hey!" Trap had been caught off guard. He and Bacon exchanged handshakes and quickly embraced. "What it do?"

"They called me and told me you were down here."

"Man, just checking out this club of yours. This place is off the chain!"

"Glad you like it."

"I see you got the old school bumping!"

"Yeah." Bacon nodded, and placed his arm on Trap's back, guiding him through the club. "After hearing that music at the bar the other night, I immediately had my DJ switch up the rotation. That shit took a brother back."

"They don't make music like they used to."

"I been thinking about starting up a record label and fixing that shit."

"That would be off the hook," Trap told him. "Inject a little old-school flavor into the market. Man, people will eat that shit up."

Bacon guided Trap up the stairs and into the club's management office. The management office had a wall of floor-to-ceiling glass windows so that one could have a panoramic view of the entire club. Bacon seated himself behind a massive desk, while Trap took in the bird's-eye view of the club.

"So, what you think about my idea of a label that puts out old school–sounding music?"

"I think it's a hit. A big hit." Trap turned and walked to the desk and took a seat opposite Bacon. "I got another moneymaking idea, too."

"Oh, yeah?" Bacon lifted an eyebrow. "What's that?"

"I want to start up a magazine. I want it to be like a real hood type of magazine, profiling niggas trying to come up on the legit side. You know, niggas in the hoods all around the country, opening up businesses and shit. No matter what it is, if you starting a business—a clothing line, a dry cleaner, a detail shop, whatever—the magazine will cover it. I just want to profile brothers and sisters doing things in the hood. Throw some fly whips in there, feature some underground musicians, authors, artists, up-and-coming muthafuckas. Add some fly cribs in there, maybe profile some cities and some projects, some vacation spots that niggas hit and some events like the Magic Show, Black Bike Week, the Kappa Beach Party and shit like that. I think it'll be a fly-ass magazine."

Bacon thought about what Trap had just proposed, then nodded. "That shit do sound fly. I'll read that bitch."

"You interested in going in on it with me?"

Again, Bacon nodded. "I might. Put me something together and I'll take a serious look at it."

"Bet."

"But in the meantime, I think we can do business on some other shit."

"Oh yeah?"

"What kinda ticket you got?"

"I'm giving up seventeen."

"I can do you fifteen five," Bacon told him.

"Thatta work?"

"Fuck it, I'll do you fifteen." Bacon allowed the numbers to dance around in his head. He knew that Trap was a baller. Judging by his jewels, his girl's jewels, their whips and their conversation, he was moving weight. That meant that he was a prize catch. If he was moving ten, or fifteen, or twenty of them thangs a month, then that meant some nice profits for him, Bacon surmised. He could be moving even more than that. And if he was moving twenty to fifty birds a month, then he was really a prize catch. So hell yeah, he would give him them thangs for fifteen.

"Fifteen?" Trap asked. *Damn*, he thought. *That price would save me two g's off of each bird.* He would definitely have to thank Laquisha for befriending Red. Fucking with this nigga Bacon was going to be a for sure win. "Shit, you got a deal."

"Speaking of the Magic Show, when's the last time you been out to Vegas?"

"Me and Quisha went about two months ago. We flew out there and gambled and just chilled."

"Man, we gonna have to hit up Vegas together. I got a little bitch that works at the Bellagio. She might have a friend for you."

Trap shrugged.

Bacon rose. "Let's go downstairs and get some drinks."

"Drinks on you?"

"You making all the money now, big-timer."

"This yo' club, I know you can hook us up with some free drinks."

"What you drinking?"

"Man, I was down in Florida with my boy about a month ago, and I fell in love with them mojitos. Yo, them joints is off the hook."

"Man, we drinking real nigga shit." Bacon laughed. "I got some Johnny Walker Black Label."

"I ain't drinking that rot-gut shit. I'm a smooth nigga."

Both men laughed.

CHAPTER THIRTY-FOUR

*L*aquisha looked around, taking in her surroundings. Red's neighborhood was filled with high-dollar mansions. A security guard stood at the gated entrance, while well-manicured, tree-lined streets welcomed visitors and residents inside. Bacon's house itself was a massive two-story French estate home. It had a pitched slate roof and a stone exterior, with cast stone accents. A large circular drive welcomed visitors to the 8,000-square-foot crib. Laquisha was definitely impressed.

Red opened the door.

"I haven't even rung the doorbell!" Laquisha said, greeting her.

"Girl, Bacon got this place rigged with cameras inside and out," Red told her. "Come on in."

Laquisha followed Red through the house and out the back door. Red had set up some champagne next to the hot tub.

"Did you bring your bathing suit?"

"I did." Laquisha smiled. "Just like you told me to."

Red stepped into the warm hot tub and sat back and relaxed. Laquisha pulled off her wrap skirt, revealing that her top was actually part of her bikini. She kicked off her flip-flops and climbed into the water with Red.

"Girl, this is what I'm talking about," Laquisha told her. "Chillaxing in a nice hot tub."

Red poured some Moët in two crystal, long-stemmed glasses. She handed Laquisha hers.

"Thank you," Laquisha said. "Girl, I love some Moët."

"Me, too. I love it better than Dom P."

"Your house is off the chain!"

Red looked around the yard. "It is nice."

"This is what I'm talking about. I've been telling Trap that we need a crib. I would love to get my hands on one like this."

"A few months ago you could have. I had this mother on the market."

"Get out of here."

"Uh-uh. I'm serious."

"Now why on earth would you sell this beautiful house?"

"A long story."

Laquisha took a sip from her champagne flute. "We got time. We just chilling."

"Girl, Bacon was locked up, and had a *Star Wars* release date before he won his appeal. There was no need for me to keep a place this big. I was going to sell it and go and get me a loft overlooking the city center."

"I hear you. But I just couldn't imagine giving up this crib. Girl, please." Laquisha shook her head. "Not me. I'da had to move somebody up in here with me, but I wouldn't be giving up my crib."

"Girl, been there and done that. I gave these bitches a place to stay and all kinds of shit happened. A jealous bitch ended up shooting up my crib, bitches was stealing and shit. It was too much drama."

"That's a shame. Give a bitch a hand, and they'll bite the muthafucka off."

Red laughed. "Girl, ain't that the truth. Hell, I might be putting this sucker back on the market."

"Girl, stop!"

"I'm serious!"

"Sell your crib?"

Red nodded. "But don't tell Bacon. I don't want it to get back to him yet."

"What's going on?"

"Nothing. I just want to ease him into the idea. We really don't need a place this big. It's just me and him."

"And what if you have kids?"

Red waved her hand over her body. "And ruin this figure? I don't think so."

Laquisha threw her head back in laughter. "Girl, you're crazy."

Both women sipped from their champagne glasses.

"I wonder if I can get Trap interested in buying it?" Laquisha said.

"You think he might?"

"I can work on him. Besides, once he sees this place he'll love it."

"Well, if you decide to do something, I'll help you. I'm also a licensed real estate agent."

"Really?"

"Yeah."

"I would have never known that."

"I love selling real estate. I don't get to do it much anymore because Bacon don't want me to work, but I own my own real estate company."

"Get the hell outta here!"

"For real, I do. I took over Schottenstein Realty after my friend died, and I changed the name to Gomez Realty. We've been rolling for a while now."

"Red, your life is so interesting."

"Girl, please. You don't know the half of it. My life is like a soap opera on steroids, mixed with three or four Lifetime movies *and* a couple of hood movies."

Laquisha laughed. "I feel you."

"Girl, I grew up in the projects, poor, and have struggled for every inch of everything that I got."

"That's why I like you, Red. You real. I could tell from the moment I met you that you wasn't no fake bitch."

"I like you, too."

"And I think Trap and Bacon done hit it off."

"Girl, them niggas is talking about going to Vegas together."

"I heard. Ain't that a bitch. And they ain't talking about taking us."

"Yeah, them dirty-dick muthafuckas is probably going down there to gamble and fuck with some bitches."

"Girl, I'll cut Trap's dick off!"

Red laughed. "As long as Bacon don't bring home nothing he ain't leave with. Just pay me, and make sure that I'm good. Don't give no bitch nothing but some dick and maybe a stick of bubblegum, and I'm good."

"You wild! Me, I'd kill Trap. I done put too much into that nigga to let another bitch get some. I'd kill his black ass."

"Hey, maybe we need to plan our own vacation."

"How about the Caribbean? Since they are going to Vegas, maybe we should go to Jamaica?"

"Or how about the Bahamas?"

"What about the Virgin Islands?"

"Trinidad and Tobago?"

"Girl, let's hit Turks and Caicos and see what Lisa Raye is up to."

"Maybe we can get us a governor."

"Girl, I would make a good first lady!"

Red lifted her leg out of the water. "I can just see myself strolling the beach and catching a fine-ass, all muscled-up Caribbean brother."

"A Dexter St. Jock, like Eddie Murphy called him!"

"Oooh, come get some first lady poohnanny."

The two of them broke into hysterical laughter. The Moët was having an effect on them.

"Girl, look at this house!" Laquisha said, examining the backyard landscaping.

"It's yours if you want to buy it."

"I'ma have to give Trap all kinds of pussy to loosen him up and get him to want to spend like this."

"The power of the pooty tang!" Red said, lifting her glass in toast.

"The power of the pooty tang!" Laquisha repeated, laughing.

CHAPTER THIRTY-FIVE

*D*etective Thomas rang the doorbell and waited patiently. He was much better prepared today than he had been the last time he visited. This time, although he was ready for the peep show, he was also determined to get to the bottom of Ezekiel's death. Something wasn't right with Raven. She didn't seem like the killer type, but in this day and age one just never knew.

He had come across many girls like her in his career; most of the time, they weren't guilty, but they could lead him directly to the guilty party. He knew that Raven knew something that she wasn't revealing, and he also knew that with a little pressure, most of the time girls like her broke down and confessed. They just needed a reason to tell what they knew, and someone to tell it to. Detective Thomas would position himself to be that some-one. He would become her friend, and in time she would open up and tell what she knew. He just needed to be in her face more often, asking questions and letting her know that this thing wasn't just going to go away. A lot of times that's what the women thought. They figured that if they could bury their heads in the sand like ostriches, things would just go away. He had to let her know that this was a murder case, and that it would be worked to the very end.

Red picked up the remote and changed the television to the security channel to see what the camera at the front entrance was monitoring. She saw that it was Detective Thomas at the front door. She had no time to run and jump in the shower again and wet herself; besides, it would be too suspicious if she were just getting out of the shower a second time. No, she needed something else. She needed to put her plan into effect immediately.

Red raced into her master bath and looked in the mirror. She needed to look like a woman who had been put through the wringer. She attacked her hair, messing it up, and then raked her hand through it trying to make it look like she'd at least tried to fix herself up. She needed puffy eyes, and maybe a reddened face. She slapped herself across her cheek as hard as she could.

"Come on, girl," she said, breathing out through her mouth. "You can take it."

She slapped herself three more times as hard as she could. Red examined herself in the mirror. Her cheeks were now a coppery red, and her eyes were watery. She looked battered.

The doorbell rang once again, and Red rushed to the door and opened it.

"Hello?" she said, sniffling.

"Oh, I was beginning to think that no one was home."

"I'm home," Red said quietly.

Detective Thomas noted a tinge of sadness in her voice. Previously she was usually more vibrant, more fiery, more energetic. He sensed there was something wrong.

"May I come in?" he asked.

Red stepped aside, allowing the detective to enter.

Thomas walked into the home and looked around. The house was filled with light because of the massive windows throughout. Each of the windows had long, golden, silky drapes that ran to the floor.

Red motioned toward the couch. "You can have a seat."

Thomas complied and Red sat across from him in the over-size La-Z-Boy.

"Did I catch you at a bad time?" Thomas asked.

"No, why?" Red ran her hand through her hair, giving herself an even more unkempt appearance.

For the first time, Thomas noticed that her face was red and that her cheeks were puffy. "What's wrong?"

"Nothing." Red looked around and fidgeted, avoiding eye contact with the detective.

"*Something's* wrong," Thomas told her, leaning forward. "Have you been crying?"

Red lowered her head and wiped away some tears. She shook her head and sniffled.

"Look, something's the matter," Thomas said, matter-of-factly. He felt that he might have created an opening. He wondered if she were crying because she knew something and wanted to tell. Perhaps it would be easier than he originally thought, he told himself.

"It's nothing," Red repeated, wiping her face again. "I'm sorry."

"Raven, if you need someone to talk to, you can talk to me. I'm a good listener."

"Thank you," she acknowledged, "but my problems aren't your problems. You being a detective and all, I'm sure you already have more than enough on your plate."

"It's never too much if I'm helping a friend. You can talk to me about anything. Whatever it is, I'll listen; I'll give you my opinion if you ask for it, and if not I'll just be a shoulder to cry on. So what's wrong?"

Red looked off into the distance. "I just have so much on my shoulders right now. I feel like I'm about to explode."

Thomas smiled. Chass told him that if he paid attention to Red, she'd fall for it. It was all about Red, he remembered Chass telling him, and he was hoping she was right. He was hoping that his listening to her would bring the confession he was waiting for.

"All my life, I've tried to please everybody, but nothing I do is good enough. People take advantage of you, they steal from you, they accuse you of things you haven't done, they beat you, they—"

"Beat you?" Thomas recoiled, interrupting her. "Who's beating you?"

Red rambled on. "You would never think that anyone close to you, who claims that they love you, would hurt you," she said meekly, not answering his question. She leaned forward, covered her face and began crying again.

Thomas exhaled. He hadn't expected this. He'd hoped that a confession was forthcoming, but now he felt bad for her. She was a beautiful woman, and no woman deserved to be beat up on by a man.

"Raven, leave him," Thomas told her. "You don't deserve this."

"And do what?" Red quizzed. "Go where?"

"Go home to your parents," Thomas suggested.

"Go home to my mother who still lives with her boyfriend who molested me when I was a child? I don't think so! She put me out of the house because he was fucking me. From six years old to ten, that man took advantage of me. I'm not going back there at all!"

Thomas felt his heart drop into his socks.

Red broke down again. "I don't have anywhere to go. Nobody to turn to."

Thomas rose, walked around the coffee table and sat himself on the arm of her chair, where he began to comfort her. "You got me, Raven. I'm here for you."

"He used to beat me for no reason," Red said softly. "It had gotten better for a while because it stopped, but then he started accusing me of sleeping with someone else and giving away our money."

Detective Thomas realized she was talking about her man now instead of her mother's boyfriend, when she mentioned money. "Giving away your money?"

Red nodded. "I swear, I haven't given away a dime. I told him a long time ago that money was missing from my account, but he didn't believe me and today he just went crazy."

Thomas shook his head. "Have you contacted the bank?"

"I did but it's the bank that's doing it."

"The bank is taking your money?"

"Well, not the bank." Red sniffled. "There's this girl who works at the bank. I know that she's the one taking my money."

"How do you know that?" Thomas asked.

"Because she hates me, and she basically confessed to doing it."

"Did you go to the bank with this?"

Red nodded her head. "I already did, but they blew me off in a major way the first time."

"What about the police? Have you contacted any law enforcement?"

"I don't know any law enforcement!" Red wailed. "You're the only cop that I know."

Detective Thomas exhaled. "Let me see what I can do. I have a friend in the bureau who may be able to help."

Red glanced up at him with her sparkling eyes. "You would do that for me?"

"Yes," he confirmed. "Nobody needs to be taken advantage of."

Red smiled softly. "Thank you."

"You're welcome, but in the meantime, you've got to get away from this guy," Thomas told her. "Domestic abuse usually ends one way, and one way only—with the funeral of the woman being beaten."

"I'm going to leave him. I need to straighten out my banking business, and then I'm going to take my money and leave him."

"Good." Thomas nodded. He rose from the arm of the chair. "I'm going to get with my buddy, and I'll get back to you today."

Red smiled her thanks.

"You get some rest," Thomas told her, walking to the door. "I'll let myself out."

Red watched as he closed the door behind him. Again, she had gotten through an interview without a single question being asked. And best of all, she thought, she now had a detective in her pocket. Life was beautiful.

CHAPTER THIRTY-SIX

*R*ed strolled into the bank, carrying an envelope filled with cash. She stood in line and waited patiently for Kera to wait on her. She even allowed two other bank patrons to go ahead of her, just so that Kera could be the one to help her.

"Next!" someone called out.

Red strolled up to Kera's window.

"I saw what you did, Red," Kera huffed when Red was in her face.

"What are you talking about?"

"You let those other ladies go ahead of you, just so I would have to be the one to wait on you. Why are you messing with me and trying my patience?"

"I'm not trying anything," Red told her. "I'm a customer and I have more than fifty thousand dollars in this bank. I can go to any line that I choose."

"Yeah, but why this one?" Kera asked. "What is it now? What

else do you want to tell me? I've been through too much torture for you to tell me anything else that will bother me, Red."

"Kera, you aren't worth torturing." Red smiled. "Everything that has happened to you, you did to yourself. You deserve the life that you have."

"My life is filled with Christ," Kera told her.

"You sacrilegious bitch. You committed the worst sins by sleeping with another chick's man, getting pregnant and then not taking care of yourself. You stupid heifer, that's child abuse. Your kid is retarded because of you and you were going to let Terry take the blame. Here I was, feeling sorry for you because she threw your monkey-ass kid and fucked him up, but you were the cause of the whole thing. Maybe dropping his ass helped him."

Kera began shaking, then spoke evilly. "Get out of my line. Now!"

"You are a servant, bitch. Serve me." Red threw her money on Kera's counter. "Now, count it, and you better not take one single penny of it like you did before."

"I didn't do shit," Kera claimed.

"Wanna bet? I got the receipt and your teller number is on it, Kera. I'm sure it won't match what was in there at that time. Now, if you want to challenge that, let's get your manager over here." Red looked around. "Manager!" she yelled.

"Shut up, Red!" Kera hissed. She held eye contact with her nemesis. Kera hated her more with each passing second.

"Count it," Red demanded.

"You need to fill out a deposit slip."

"I ain't filling out a damn thing. You fill it out for me," Red told her. "You helped yourself to my shit before. Do it now."

"Red, don't make me . . ."

"Bitch, don't make you what?" Red asked, cutting her off. "Don't make you lose your job and get yo' ass whooped all in the same day?"

"Account number please?" Kera asked, not wanting to draw any more attention to what was happening.

"You know it already."

Kera looked at her and squinted her eyes. "I need to see your ID."

"It's a cash deposit, you dumb bitch. Deposit, get that? You don't need an ID with a deposit. And I'm in your face . . . that's all the ID you need."

Kera huffed, and counted out Red's money. It was $10,000. "You are aware that deposits over seven thousand dollars have to be reported to the IRS?"

Red shrugged. "Do your job, teller."

Kera printed up Red's receipt and handed it to her. "Thank you. Have a nice day."

Red snatched the receipt, spun and marched out of the bank. Back at her Navigator, Detective Thomas was waiting for her.

"So, how did it go?"

Red nodded. "It went okay."

"What do you think is going to happen?" Thomas asked.

"We'll see."

Red and Thomas climbed into her Navigator.

"While we're waiting, I have some questions to ask you about Ezekiel Morrison," Thomas told her.

"Go ahead." Red nodded.

"You were the last one to see Ezekiel alive, were you not?"

Red shrugged. "I don't know. I mean, I thought that Q would have been."

"Q? As in Quentin Carter?"

Red nodded.

"Why do you assume Mr. Carter saw him last?"

"Q supposedly found him, right?"

"Why do you say supposedly?" Detective Thomas shifted in his seat. "What are you trying to say, Raven?"

"I'm just saying." Red became frustrated and exhaled. She rested her forehead in the palm of her hand.

"What, Raven? What are you saying?" Thomas asked, putting on the pressure.

"Okay, look. I'm not saying that Q did anything, but me and Q, we were together back then."

Thomas nodded. "Go on."

"Well, Zeke, he was jealous, and he wanted to get with me."

"Are you saying that you had a relationship with Ezekiel?"

"Fuck no!" Red declared. "I don't even roll like that."

"Okay . . ."

"He came over that day and tried to grab my ass," Red told him. "He was drunk, and things got out of hand. He got violent and like all the men in my life, he tried to beat me up and force himself on me."

Thomas sat quietly and waited for Red to continue.

"Q called him, and I snatched his phone and told him that Zeke was trying to rape me. I assumed that Q was on his way, but I managed to get away from Zeke before Q got there."

"So you left, and Quentin rushed there to save you from a drunken Ezekiel?"

"Yes." She looked him in his eyes.

Detective Thomas exhaled. It all made sense to him now. He was suspicious of Raven, when he should have been looking at Quentin, but he and Ezekiel were friends, supposedly. Had Quentin been mad enough to kill Ezekiel? Wouldn't the average man be mad enough to kill over his girlfriend? Quentin had had enough time before the police arrived to do something to Ezekiel. The case had definitely taken a twist, that was for certain, Thomas thought.

CHAPTER THIRTY-SEVEN

Kera punched out at the time clock and headed for her car. She was now rolling in a Toyota Camry, thanks to the money she had been stealing from Red. And now, she was about to help herself to another nice chunk. Listening to Mary Mary's "God in Me," she drove to another bank branch to make a withdrawal. She didn't realize how easy or how addictive it would become. She remembered when Bacon rolled up on her asking about Red. She was nervous to give him the money from Red's account, but when she saw how easy it was, it became a habit to skim.

When Red came into the bank and began depositing money again, Kera assumed she was back with Bacon, so Kera started taking her percentage off the top. Kera called it a handling fee.

She zipped her car into a parking space and headed inside, hoping that none of the employees recognized her from the other branch.

Then she filled out her withdrawal slip and waited patiently in line. Red had deposited a total of $10,000, and she was going to sting her for two g's. Twenty percent of the take. A fair fee for her.

Kera felt a twinge of satisfaction when she realized how much she had gotten away with. She knew not to take too much, but just enough. *That bitch got so much money, she can't even tell it's gone*, Kera said to herself as the second person in front of her went to a teller. Kera knew that Red didn't check her account often because she relied on what the bank statement said as truth and kept steppin', so Kera felt no remorse in doing what she was doing. Kera remembered how Red taxed her for living at her home and then put her out. *She deserves everything she gets*, Kera's mind told her. *She owes me for a lifetime's worth of misery and she wasn't even my real friend. I hope she dies broke, that bitch.*

Kera was next in line and pulled out the fake ID she had made with Red's name on it. She made it on her computer and laminated it as if it were the real thing. Kera was proud of her skills.

"Next!" a teller called out.

Kera nonchalantly stepped to the window. "Good afternoon," she said, trying to divert the teller's attention.

"Good afternoon," the teller replied.

Kera continued to make small talk as she handed over the withdrawal slip and her ID. This was the moment of truth and it always made her nervous, no matter how many times she did it. She found herself shaking slightly.

"Thank you, Ms. Gomez," the teller said, handing the ID back to her.

The teller counted out $2,000 in front of Kera and handed it to her in an envelope, along with a receipt.

"Anything else I can do for you?" the teller asked.

"No, thank you," Kera said. "You have a blessed day."

"You, too," the teller replied.

Kera turned and headed for the exit. Happily, she bounced toward her car.

"Ooh, excuse me," she said, bumping one of four men in dark suits. She tried to maneuver around them until one of the men spoke.

"Excuse me, miss. FBI." He flashed a badge. "May I have a word with you?"

"Oh, my God!" Kera proclaimed. Her knees almost buckled.

"Could you step back inside the bank with us, please?" another agent asked. Kera wanted to run but she was surrounded.

She was led back into the bank amidst stares and into a side office where her purse was confiscated.

"May I see your identification, please?" an agent asked.

"Um . . . It's in my wallet," Kera said nervously. "May I ask what this is about?"

An agent handed Kera her wallet and she didn't know what to do. She didn't know whether to pull out her own ID, or the fake one. She decided that since she just made a withdrawal, her receipt and ID should match, so she handed the agent the fake ID.

The FBI agent handed the ID to another gentleman, who examined it briefly.

"It's a fake," Detective Thomas told the agents.

"No, it's not!" Kera protested.

"What's your name, young lady?" he asked.

Confidently, she said, "My name is Raven Gomez!"

Detective Thomas laughed. "If you're Raven Gomez, then who is this?"

The men stepped aside, and Red walked into the office, smiling at Kera.

"You always wanted to be me, didn't you?" Red pursed her lips and shook her head.

Kera looked between the men and Red and began crying.

"The rest of the identification in your purse has another name," an agent advised her.

"Miss Gomez"—an agent looked at Red—"did you give this person permission to use your name or give her access to your personal banking information?"

"Hell no," Red answered.

The agent turned to Kera. "Miss, are you aware that it's a felony offense to impersonate another person and steal money from his or her bank account?"

"I'm sorry," Kera wailed. "Please don't take me to prison. Red, please tell them it was a mistake!"

"I want to press charges to the fullest extent of the law," Red said, a satisfied smirk on her face. "Who do I give my statement to?"

"You can do it with me, downtown," Thomas told her.

"What's going to happen to her?" Red asked.

"She'll be arrested and taken to a federal detention facility until she can be arraigned by a federal magistrate in a day or two," an agent explained while handcuffing Kera.

"Oh, so she is going to jail?"

"She's going to prison for a long time," another agent said. "We got her on surveillance making the transaction, we caught her with the fake ID and we detained her with the money. This is a rock-solid case."

Kera lowered her head and really started bawling now.

Red turned to Kera. "All of this is because of you. If you would have left that letter where it was, none of this would have happened, but you couldn't leave well enough alone, you jealous-hearted bitch. I hope you have fun in prison, you self-righteous whore. You'll be praying to the Lord, all right, in there. Just give it up freely, Kera, it's less painful."

Red strutted out of the office. One bitch down.

CHAPTER THIRTY-EIGHT

*K*era's deception gave Red an idea. She needed to square her business with Triple Crown, because she had Bacon signing contracts and too many people in the mix. She needed to set things up so that only she could talk to Triple Crown, and only she could negotiate and sign contracts. There were too many Lisa Lennoxes in the mix, and she needed to limit the number to one.

Since the idea hit her, Red had hit the library, the video store and a few other places and established IDs and accounts under the name Lisa Lennox. She needed to get hooked up with a connect so that she could get a fake ID under that name as well. The fake ID wouldn't pass muster with the cops she knew, but for ordinary people in everyday situations it would work just fine. But first, she went to the county courthouse to get a doing-business-as license (DBA) under the name Lisa Lennox.

Then she would be able to open a bank account in that name, and get a debit card. That would open up a whole other line of identification that she would be able to access. Phone bills, utility bills, you name it . . . all under the name Lisa Lennox. She would become the real Lisa, and thus cut everyone else out. It would help to have a second identification when she did the things that she was planning to do—especially if she decided to change locations and needed to hide her true identity.

Red filled out the DBA form and waited patiently for the clerk to call her to the counter.

"May I help you?" the clerk asked.

Red stepped to the counter, and slid the form to the clerk.

"You want to establish a DBA?" the clerk asked.

"Yes." Red nodded.

"Five dollars," the clerk told her.

Five dollars, Red thought. It was only going to take five measly dollars to change her life around and become another person? It wasn't a legal name change, but it was good enough for what she needed. She was going to be able to legally conduct business and enter into contracts under the name Lisa Lennox.

Red handed the clerk a $5 bill and watched as he typed the info into his computer, legally registering her to do business in that name. Her plan was well on its way to succeeding. Kera was out of the way and Bacon would be soon. By the time she was finished, she was going to be even with everyone on her shit list.

The clerk handed Red the papers and her receipt. She gathered up her documents, slid them in a folder and flounced out of the county clerk's office. She was going to secure her TCP money and her new career as an author, and she was finally going to be able to give herself the life that she wanted, without having to depend on a man to give it to her. She was now using her head instead of her body, and it felt good to her.

• • •

Detective Thomas strolled into the rehab facility and found Chass sitting with Q, who was now using a cane but was still walking with a limp.

Q's recovery had taken everybody by surprise.

"Well, well, well," Thomas told him. "You look like a new man."

"I feel like one." Q smiled, turning around slowly and sitting down on his bed.

"And how are you doing?" Detective Thomas asked Chass.

"I'm fine." Chass smiled, proud of Quentin's ongoing recovery. "What brings you by here?"

"Actually, I'm here to see Mr. Carter."

"About what?" Chass asked. She went from smiling to serious in 15 seconds flat.

"Just some questions about Mr. Morrison." Thomas smiled.

"You came down here to see my client without my permission?" Chass frowned.

"I'm still a detective," Thomas told her. "I have a job to do."

"And I'm still his attorney, and the law is still the law, and you can't question him without me being present."

"You are present."

"But you didn't know that."

"Where else would you be?" Detective Thomas questioned. "It's obvious that you and your client have something going on besides legal consulting."

"Watch it, Detective," Chass said sternly.

Thomas held up his hands in surrender. "Look, I just have a few questions. It won't take long."

Chass was still pissed off about the tapes and the fact that Quentin was trying to protect Red. Under other circumstances, she would have let the detective question him, but the only reason she continued her line of questioning was to be nosy.

"What do you want to ask me?" Q asked.

"I wanted to ask you about the day you found Ezekiel," Thomas told him. "You went back to your apartment for what reason?"

"Because I live there." Q smiled.

"And for no other reason?" Thomas asked, lifting an eyebrow.

"He answered the question," Chass told him. "Move on, Detective."

"Had you talked to Ezekiel that day?" Thomas asked.

"No."

"Had you called him?"

"He didn't answer."

"He didn't answer?"

"If you're going to ask me the same questions over and over after I've answered you, this is going to take a really long time," Q told him.

"Did anyone answer his phone?" Thomas asked.

"No," Q said, shaking his head.

"So, there was no particular reason you went back to your apartment that day?" Thomas asked.

Q shook his head.

"When was the last time you spoke with Raven, prior to discovering Ezekiel unconscious?"

"Earlier that day," Q told him. "Before I left."

"What was Ezekiel's relationship with Raven like?" Thomas asked.

"They hated each other."

"Did you ever suspect that Ezekiel might want to have sexual relations with Raven?"

Q shrugged. "It wouldn't have surprised me. Most men wanted to."

Detective Thomas couldn't hate on Q's response. He had masturbated several times since seeing Red put oil on her body that day. The coconut scent lingered in his nostrils every time he thought about it. He wanted her just as bad as the next man.

"You ever hear them argue?" Thomas asked.

"They hated each other," Q repeated. "Zeke thought she was scandalous and he didn't want me with her. You don't think Red had something to do with Zeke's death, do you?"

Detective Thomas shrugged. Either Q was a pretty good actor, or he had nothing to do with Ezekiel's death. Something wasn't right. The toxicology reports all suggested a poisonous combination of chemicals and alcohol in Ezekiel's system. If Raven hadn't killed him, and Quentin hadn't killed him, there was only one other possibility.

"Was there any change in Ezekiel's behavior?" the detective asked. "Any signs that something was upsetting him?"

"Zeke wasn't the type to commit suicide, if that's what you're getting at."

"Quentin, I'm afraid that there is no certain type who does or doesn't commit suicide," Thomas told him. "In my career, I've seen guys who you would least expect to commit suicide, kill themselves. Guys with good looks, great careers, great-looking wives and tons of money in the bank, just blow their brains out one morning without leaving so much as a note. You never know."

Q shook his head. "Naw, Zeke didn't go out like that."

Detective Thomas rose. He would have to keep digging, he told himself. If Q and Zeke argued, then why hide it? If he had gone there to kill Zeke, then that would be a reason to hide it. What if Zeke was already dead when he got there and Quentin was just covering up for Raven? There were just too many variables, too many questions.

If Ezekiel wasn't suicidal, then that meant he was poisoned. Men usually didn't poison other men. If Q had stormed in there to rescue Raven, then the two of them would have fought. However, if Ezekiel was trying to rape Raven, then the two of them would have struggled, and she wouldn't have had time to poison him. Unless her rape story was bogus. He was going to have to pressure her some more. Her story just didn't sound right. There were still too many pieces missing.

CHAPTER THIRTY-NINE

*R*ed picked up her cell phone and dialed the number to Triple Crown. A receptionist answered.

"Triple Crown Publications is the blueprint," the receptionist answered with a smile in her voice. "How may I direct your call?"

"Yes, may I speak with Kammi Johnson, please?"

"Who may I say is calling?"

"Lisa Lennox."

"Are you one of the authors?"

"Yes, I am."

"Hold one minute, please."

Red listened to the clicks and beeps as she was transferred to another extension.

"Hello, this is Kammi," a voice chimed.

"Hi, Kammi, this is Lisa Lennox."

"Oh, hi, Lisa. How have you been?"

"I've been doing well," Red told her. "How have you been?"

"Busy, busy, busy," Kammi told her. "Getting ready for some big releases, the BEA and just running around like a chicken with its head cut off."

Red laughed. "I hear you. I can understand busy."

"Your novel is doing well."

"Really?" Red said excitedly.

"It's still number one on the *Essence* bestsellers list."

"Yeah, that's good news!" Red told her.

"We can't wait to see part two."

"I'm working on it."

"Well, you don't have much time," Kammi told her. "Your deadline is approaching fast."

"I know."

"We need to get with either Vida or Keith and finalize a cover design. Have you thought about what you want?"

"I was picturing using the same cover, and just putting Part Two on it."

"That usually works best," Kammi agreed. "That way people will know that the books are related. A lot of times they'll pick both part one and part two up at the store when they see the covers are closely related."

"Then I'll go with that."

"Can you give me a sneak peek into what you have so far?" Kammi asked excitedly.

"I want it to be a surprise," Red lied.

"I can't wait. I just loved the first book. I don't really say this to many of my authors, but I am a fan. Your book was so real, so street, so exciting. I'm dying to read part two."

"It's coming."

"Did you get the check?"

"I did," Red told her. "Thank you."

"If this project turns out to be a success like the first one, you need to start planning for your long-term career."

"Like how?"

"Like, start thinking about a three-book deal with Triple Crown."

"A three-book deal!" Red said excitedly. She had just done a one-book deal with a $50,000 advance. Was Kammi talking about three books for $150,000? If so, she could really get into this writing stuff. She had to make sure that she had this money on lock.

"Yeah, I was just talking to the boss lady herself," Kammi added. "She is very pleased with your sales numbers."

"That is the best news that I've heard all day!" Red said ecstatically.

"Well, just hurry up and get us your next book."

"I will," Red told her.

"Great."

"Kammi, the reason I was calling today was because I found an agent."

"Oh, good for you."

"I know. She's great."

"Finding an agent is as hard as getting a publishing deal," Kammi told her. "Agents don't take on new clients often."

"That's what I heard," Red said.

"But then again, you have a pretty good track record now," Kammi told her. "So, who is your agent?"

"Her name is Raven Gomez."

"Raven Gomez?"

"Yes. I've started the Raven Gomez Literary Agency."

"Well, good for you!" Kammi laughed. "Congratulations on your new business."

"Well, I figured that no one can represent me like me, and while I'm at it, I might as well take on other clients as well. Finding an agent is hard, so why not open up doors for others as well as myself?"

"That's a great way to look at it. Are you going to relocate?"

"I'm thinking about it."

"That wouldn't be a bad move. You know, this business is really a face-to-face business, with a lot of meetings and lots of lunches. Being an agent means wining and dining editors and attending industry functions, most of which take place in New York."

"I know," Red told her. "I figure I can fly back and forth for now, and rely on my phone, fax and e-mail to get a lot of things done."

"Well, I'll put you down as the agent of record."

"Great, and make sure that all of the checks go to my agency's new PO box, which I'll e-mail you. And make sure that all contact regarding Lisa Lennox or inquiries into any advances or contracts are forwarded to me. I don't want any information given out. I want to handle it personally."

"I'll make a note of that in the Lisa Lennox file."

"Thanks, Kammi."

Red hung up and leaned back in her chair with a shit-eating grin on her face. She had just cut Bacon out of the game. Now, she just had one more phone call to make. This one would be a great pleasure. It was now time to get even with that bitch Terry for shooting up her crib.

CHAPTER FORTY

*H*ello, Social Services, how many I direct your call?"

"I need the Child Welfare Division, please."

"One moment please."

Red listened patiently to the music as her call was being transferred. Suddenly, a woman came on the line.

"Child Protective Services, this is Rhonda, how may I help you?"

"Hi, Rhonda. I need to speak with an investigator."

"I'm an enforcement agent. How may I help you?"

"I wanted to report a severe case of child abuse."

"Child abuse? How old is the child?"

"About six to eight months."

"Six to eight months?"

"Yes," Red confirmed. She could hear Rhonda tapping away at her keyboard.

"Are you a relative, a teacher, a neighbor?"

"I'm a family member."

"Is the child in your custody?"

"No, unfortunately. He's in the custody of his drug-dealing father and his abusive girlfriend."

"Have you notified law enforcement?"

"No."

"Is the child in any immediate danger?"

"Yes!" Red snapped. "The child is being molested."

"Oh, my God," Rhonda proclaimed. "And you said this was a baby?"

"Yes."

"Are you able to dial 911 at this time?"

"So the parents can pretend like everything is fine? The police won't take the baby away if there are no physical signs of abuse."

"Why do you say the child is in immediate danger?"

"The child is specially challenged, and the father slaps him around," Red told her. "I saw it with my own eyes on several occasions. I also personally witnessed the sickest act in my entire life: I saw the father's girlfriend stick the baby's penis in her mouth."

"Oh, my God!" Rhonda exclaimed again. She absolutely detested child molesters, and would personally shoot each and every one of them if she could. Hurting a child was so evil and sadistic and those who did it deserved to die the most torturous deaths imaginable in her book.

"Please, you have to hurry up and get this child away from them," Red said. She pretended to be crying. "They are evil people. The girlfriend is under psychiatric care; the father is a major drug dealer who blames the baby for being challenged, so he abuses the child."

"I am personally going to launch this investigation and look into this myself," Rhonda reassured her.

"Thank you," Red said, sniffling.

"Would you be willing to give a statement?"

"Of course!"

"What is your name, ma'am?"

"Vivica Borrego," Red lied.

"And what are the names of the parents or parent of the child?"

"The father's name is Mekel Simmons and the girlfriend's name is Terry Washington. Actually there are other kids there too, and if this is happening to the baby, Lord only knows what's happening with the others."

"Well, now they have me in their lives, and I love sending people like this to prison for a long long time."

Bacon strolled into the room. "What up, Red?" He walked up to Red and kissed her forehead.

"Where you going, sweetie?"

"I gotta go out and take care of that thing."

"What thing?"

"You know," Bacon said, pulling her close and kissing her again. "Blue taking a shipment back to New York for me tonight."

"Oh."

"I gotta find my white polo shirt with the beige and brown stripes," Bacon told her.

"It's in the dryer, why?"

"I'ma pack and head to New York for a couple of days. I'll be back on Sunday. Can you maintain that long without me?"

"I'll try." Red smiled. "So, why you going to New York?"

"Get some business straight. Then we gonna head to Philly and meet with some cats. I might have a window into Philly. If I can start supplying them cats with some of this fire that Juan has been sending me, we might be living up the Trump Tower this time next year."

"Can I go to New York with you?"

"Not this time. This is business. I don't want you nowhere around the shit we transporting, but I promise, next time you can go."

"You want me to pack you a bag?" Red asked sadly.

"Yeah, I just need enough clothes to last till Sunday," Bacon told her. "What you gon' do while I'm gone?"

"You know me . . . shop, maybe get a new whip . . ."

"What you trying to buy?"

"I'ma trade in all my cars and just buy one," Red told him. "I want a new Range Rover."

"Hell, if you trading everything else in, then you should be able to get it for nothing."

"Can I push your new Bentley to the dealership?"

"Damn, girl, you killing me!" Bacon laughed. "Yeah, you can push it, just don't try to trade my shit in. You know how to drop the top on it?"

"I'll figure it out."

"All right." Bacon slapped her on her ass. "Go and pack me some clothes so I can get outta here."

CHAPTER FORTY-ONE

*R*ed couldn't stand having Bacon's smell on her. Before he left, he tried to get some pussy for the road, but she couldn't give him any. She didn't want to because of what she heard Foxy say in the salon. The thought of Bacon fucking a transvestite sickened Red. As far as she was concerned Bacon was gay, and if it were up to her, he would never touch her again.

Red dried off from her shower and threw on a T-shirt and a pair of capris. She had a nice pair of sandals to match. She threw her hair up in a ponytail, then climbed into Bacon's Bentley to start the other phase of her plan. Everything was coming together nicely and she had only a few more to pay back.

She picked up the phone and made a phone call. "I need to see you right away, please . . . hurry." She hung the phone up, then sat down and waited.

Twenty minutes later, the doorbell rang, and Red rushed to her front door and opened it. Detective Thomas was standing before her.

"Hi."

"Hi." Red smiled. She surreptitiously looked at the corner ceiling to make sure that the tiny red light on the camera was on. "Come on in." Red stepped to the side and allowed him inside, then closed the door.

"What's the big emergency?" Thomas asked.

"No emergency."

"I rushed over here," he told her. "You didn't sound too happy."

"I'm sorry if I made you think that," Red apologized. "I'm very happy."

Detective Thomas stopped and stared at Red. She was the most beautiful creature he had ever laid eyes on. Life had damaged her, but she was still redeemable. *She could still be wife material*, he mused. He thought about the life he could give her if only she turned out to be innocent, but in order to know that, he would have to get her to come clean. Why didn't Raven understand that he could really help her if she let him?

"So, what can I do for you today, Ms. Gomez?"

Red smiled at him and he got lost in her eyes. Her flawless red-toned skin contrasted greatly with her hazel-green eyes, setting them off.

"I just wanted to say thank you for everything that you've done for me," Red told him.

She leaned forward and kissed Detective Thomas on his lips. It shocked him at first but then he looked into her eyes and watched her face transform. What had been an innocent kiss was followed by a second kiss, this one slower, more passionate.

"Oh, my God, I'm sorry," Red told him and turned away, feigning embarrassment. "You must think I'm—"

"No, it's no problem," Thomas interrupted her. He paused for a moment, then spoke her name. "Raven?"

Timidly, Red turned back toward him.

"I think that you're the most beautiful woman I've ever seen in my life. I've been wanting to tell you this since I first met you. You're like no other woman I've ever come across."

Detective Thomas caressed the side of Red's face. She leaned forward and again their lips locked. Their tongues found each other, slowly at first, but more assuredly as the kiss progressed and their tongues danced together. She smelled like jasmine and white roses to him, while he smelled of clover and spice to her.

Red pulled the detective farther inside, kissing him passionately while backing her way to the sofa. Detective Thomas tossed off his jacket while Red unbuttoned his shirt. He lifted Red into the air, kissing her passionately the entire time.

"I can make you happy," Thomas murmured. "Just let me make you happy."

Red pulled off Thomas's shirt and T-shirt, tossing them both to the floor. Thomas kicked off his shoes and Red unbuckled his trousers, allowing them to fall to the floor as well. She grabbed his enlarged manhood and slowly stroked him up and down. *This is going to be a nice lay,* she thought. The detective was packing a nice-size pistol in his underwear.

Detective Thomas pulled down Red's capris and pulled off her T-shirt. She tossed aside her bra, and stepped out of her panties as well. Detective Thomas lost his socks and underwear. Completely naked, the two of them locked into an entwining embrace that would make a pair of mating boa constrictors jealous.

The detective fell back onto the couch and Red fell on top of him. Locking eyes with him, she straddled his body, took his penis in her hand and slid it into her.

"Oh, shit!" Thomas cried out at the sensation of entering into Red's tight pussy.

It had been a while since Red had some dick so she was going to enjoy this. She slid up and down on Thomas's thick, stiff shaft, rotating her hips and grinding against him like a professional whore.

Thomas sucked in air, moaning, almost coming to tears at the feeling of Red's tightness. She tightened her pussy each time she slid down on his tool, causing his toes to curl. He hadn't felt pussy like that in all his years, and to top it off, Red was moaning and crying out like he was hurting her. Her sound alone made him want to cum.

"Oh, oh, oh," Red moaned with each of her strokes. "Oh, God! Oh!"

Red ground, and rotated and slid up and down on Detective Thomas until he couldn't control himself any longer.

"Raven, for God's sake, stop!"

She worked her pussy harder.

"I'm cumming!" he shouted.

"Oh baby, me, too!"

He gushed up inside of Red like an exploding volcano releasing hot, thick lava. His penis seemed to harden and expand even more while he released the pressure. Red's own juices slid down his manhood as she came with him.

Breathing heavily, a sweaty Red collapsed onto the spent detective.

"Oh, my God, Raven," Thomas said, gasping for air. "I've never cum like that before."

Red caressed the side of his face. "Damn, you were good."

"I can't believe we just did that."

Red laughed. "I can. I've been wanting this for a while."

"You know this changes everything." Thomas's expression grew somber.

"Like what?"

"I can't leave you here. I want you by my side. I can't let another man have you. Leave this clown and move in with me."

Red shook her head and turned away. Gathering her composure, she turned back to him.

"Give me time, Detective. I need to stand on my own so I can think about my life."

Feeling slightly dejected, Thomas nodded. "That's fair enough, but I want you to know something. I have some serious feelings for you, Raven."

"I have feelings for you, too," she lied, swallowing hard.

"Will you at least do me a favor and leave him tonight?" Thomas asked.

"He's not coming back tonight."

"Why not? Where is he?"

"He went to New York."

"New York? What'd he go to New York for?"

Red turned and stared off into space. Her silence filled the room.

"Raven," Thomas said, touching her shoulder. "I can't help you, unless you let me."

Red nodded. "He's transporting a truck full of drugs. Him and his friend Blue, and two other guys."

"Are you serious?" Thomas asked.

Red nodded and started crying. "They're in a rented Mustang, following the dope in a Ryder truck. The dope is in the fake sidewalls of the truck."

"How in the hell did you get mixed up with this guy?" Thomas asked angrily. "Do you realize you could be named as an accessory in a conspiracy?"

"He said that he would kill me if I ever told," Red sobbed.

Detective Thomas caressed her hair. "Don't worry about that now."

"You don't know Bacon, he's dangerous."

"You don't have anything to worry about now," Thomas reassured her. "I'll take care of everything."

Red hugged the detective, so he couldn't see the smirk that crept across her face. She was counting on him taking care of Bacon. Fair exchange ain't robbery.

CHAPTER FORTY-TWO

*D*riving Bacon's Bentley, Red thought about what she was supposed to be doing. She had tied her hair up into a ponytail and now rode through the city with the top down, enjoying the breeze tussling with her hair. She planned to go to the mall, shop for a while and end her day with a relaxing spa treatment at one of the shops uptown, but she had one more stop to make.

Red walked into the community hospital and looked around for the information desk. She hated hospitals. The smells of antiseptics, urine and hint of death lingered in the air. Red located the area she was looking for and headed toward it through automatic doors. She walked up to a desk where two women were chatting.

"May I help you?" one of the ladies asked her.

"Yes, I need to see a doctor."

"Is this an emergency, ma'am?"

"Yes, you stupid bitch!" Red snapped. "Why else would I be here . . . to listen to the fucking hospital music?"

The other woman who had been chatting with the clerk abruptly walked off. A chill ran down the spine of the woman Red snapped at. Looking at her closely, the woman spoke again. "I'm sorry, ma'am. What is your emergency?"

"I've been raped."

The woman hightailed it into overdrive. She picked up the phone and spoke some type of medical lingo into it, then spoke to Red. "Come with me, please." She escorted her into an examination room.

A nurse came into the room and began questioning Red.

"Are you bleeding? Are you in any pain?"

Red stared at her as if she were retarded.

"We're here to help you. Please take this." The nurse handed Red a thin paper gown. She tried to help Red get undressed but Red declined her help.

"I can do it," she barked.

The nurse looked at Red. "I'm just trying to help."

"I don't need your help."

This time the nurse glared at Red. "Get undressed completely, and a doctor will be with you immediately." She left the room.

Red did as she was instructed, slid into the paper gown and eased up on the examining table, awaiting the doctor.

A young physician walked into the room accompanied by the nurse she kicked out.

"Hi, my name is Dr. Blakely, how are you tonight?"

"Not good," Red mustered, quietly. "I've been—"

"I know," the doctor confirmed. "I'm so sorry to hear about your circumstances, but rest assured, I want you to know that we're going to take really good care of you. Is there anyone you want us to call?"

Red shook her head. "I don't have anyone to call."

"Well, a counselor will be in here in a moment to speak to

you. We have a police officer who is going to speak with you in a little while as well. Is that okay?"

Red nodded. She used every bit of willpower that she could conjure up to keep from beaming. A police report was going to be perfect.

"You mind if I take a look?" the doctor asked.

"Sure, Doctor."

Dr. Blakely pulled on a pair of sterile surgical gloves and walked to the table.

"Are you able to scoot down some?"

"I . . . I need help." Red looked at the nurse. She wanted to burst out in laughter because the nurse rolled her eyes at Red. The nurse helped Red move her bottom to the edge of the examination table in a rough manner and stood by the tray of sterile instruments so she could hand them to the physician.

The doctor lifted up Red's paper gown and began to examine her vaginal area.

"Looks a little red."

The nurse knew the drill. She pulled on some surgical gloves, opened the rape kit and handed the doctor a long, thin cotton swab.

Dr. Blakely took the swab, parted Red's vagina and examined it. Her vaginal canal was red, indicating intercourse. He swabbed deep inside her, pulling out the cotton covered in semen. He handed it to the nurse, who handed him another cotton swab. Dr. Blakely repeated the procedure.

The nurse placed the cotton swabs in separate plastic bags for the lab.

"I'm going to flush you. It will feel like a douche except this is a little more powerful. This solution is antibacterial, and it is spermicidal. Are you on any type of birth control?"

"Yes." Red nodded. There was no way in hell she would have

let Detective Thomas cum in her pussy if she weren't on any birth control.

The doctor inserted a tube into her vaginal canal and squeezed some solution into her, cleansing her insides. It felt cool and tingly. Almost erotic. Red lifted her head and back up off the table a bit as the cooling liquid gushed up inside her.

Doctor Blakely examined Red once again. "You aren't torn anywhere, and the abrasions that you sustained will go away in time. Are you in any pain?"

"Just a little sore down there."

The doctor examined her arms and neck. "No bruises. Tell me if this hurts." He pressed against her ribs, her back and her chest.

"No, no pain," Red told him.

The doctor squeezed her thigh. "Any pain here?"

Again Red shook her head.

The doctor held up his hand. "How many fingers am I holding up?"

"Two."

"Squeeze my fingers."

Red squeezed the doctor's two fingers.

"Good. Anything you need? Any pain?"

"That stuff you took out of me? Was that semen?"

The doctor nodded.

"And the police will be able to use that as evidence?"

"Yes. DNA is always the best evidence. You ready to talk to the officer?"

"Yes, Doctor."

He helped Red sit up and gave her a blanket to cover up with while she spoke with the authorities.

The nurse stepped out of the room and returned with two uniformed police officers and a plainclothes detective.

"Hello, ma'am. I'm Detective Baldwin, this is Officer Johns, and this is Officer Sanford. Are you okay?"

Red tensed up, and cowered in front of them.

"Officer Johns is a forensic technician," Detective Baldwin explained. "She is going to collect DNA evidence from your person. She is going to use a special tape, and place it on you and then pull it off. If the perp left any physical evidence, then we'll pick it up on the tape. Any clothing fibers, skin follicles, hair follicles, sweat or other DNA evidence is going to help the investigation."

"I know who it is."

"Do you?" Detective Baldwin asked, raising his eyebrow.

"Yes." Red nodded.

The detective pulled out his notepad. "You have a name?"

Red looked around at each of them. "Yeah, he's one of you."

"Excuse me?" Officer Johns asked.

"The muthafucka was a cop," Red said.

A deafening silence crashed in the room as the officers contemplated the bomb that she had just dropped on them.

CHAPTER FORTY-THREE

*P*ass the muthafuckin' blunt, nigga!" Bacon turned to Blue, taking his eyes off the road for a moment.

He and Blue were in the Mustang following Blue's homeboys Corey and Cavi, who were driving the truck.

"Bump that new Eminem, nigga!" Blue said, turning up the volume on the stereo.

"It's a damn factory system, fool!" Bacon said, laughing. "It ain't gon' beat."

"Nigga, my dude in the studio said that 50 Cent is coming out with a new CD that goes hard," Blue told him. "He said we ain't gonna believe that shit."

"That nigga 50 always go hard."

Blue grabbed the blunt from Bacon and took a long pull. His lungs became so full of the marijuana smoke that he started coughing.

"Damn, this some good shit!" Blue declared.

"That's that Peruvian shit right there," Bacon told him.

"Where you get that shit from?"

"I got a weed connection out of this world!" Bacon bragged. "Nigga, you know my dope connection is strong. My weed connection put that other shit to shame!"

Neither paid attention to the highway patrolman sitting on the side of the road as they broke into laughter. The patrolman pulled out and turned on his lights in an attempt to catch them.

"Shit!" Bacon shouted as he looked into his rearview mirror.

"What?"

"Nigga, I got a one-time coming up on my tail."

"Damn!" Blue said, stomping the floor. "We got some blunts and some heat."

"Roll down the window so the smoke can get out," Bacon told him.

Blue rolled down the window. "Here that fool comes. Damn, we wasn't speeding."

"Man, I don't want to go to jail tonight. Especially for no weed and no burners!" Bacon declared.

"If that fool starts tripping, I'll eat these blunts," Blue said, holding up four fat, rolled cigars.

Bacon pulled the Mustang to the side of the road when the police officer got behind him. To his relief, the trooper swerved around him but his relief quickly disappeared when the trooper pulled up behind the van that was carrying his drugs.

"No! No! No!" Bacon shouted, banging his fists on the steering wheel. "Pull *me* over instead!"

"Goddamn!" Blue yelled.

The trooper stayed behind the van, which slowly pulled over to the side of the road.

"Them fools wasn't speeding," Blue declared. "They was going the same speed as us."

"Them niggas must of been doing something else," Bacon told him. "You think them fools was drinking and he saw 'em?"

Blue shrugged. "Man, them niggas know better. I hope they wasn't."

Bacon decided to get back into traffic not to appear suspicious. They drove past the pulled-over truck.

"We can just wait for them fools up here at the next rest stop," Blue suggested.

Traffic slowed ahead of them, and eventually it came to a crawl and then a stop.

"At least this will give them fools a chance to catch up to us," Bacon admitted.

The rear door of the U-Haul just in front of Bacon and Blue slid open, and out poured several men with blue windbreakers with the letters FBI stenciled on them.

"Freeze!" several of the agents shouted, pointing guns at the Mustang.

"What the fuck?" Bacon shouted. He lifted his hands in the air.

"Damn!" Blue shouted, also lifting his hands in the air.

The agents surrounded the Mustang, and Blue and Bacon soon found themselves lying facedown on the highway being handcuffed.

"This is bullshit!" Bacon shouted. "What the fuck is going on here?"

"You don't know?" One of the agents who'd cuffed them laughed.

"Know what?" Bacon asked.

"We taking you back to where your homies are."

"What homies?" Bacon asked. "I don't know what you talking about."

"Man, why let them have all the fun?" the agent sad. "Let's head back down to where the truck is, and we'll all watch together as we pull down those fake sidewalls and see what's there."

Bacon's heart and spirits sank. He was busted. The feds knew exactly where the dope was, which told him that he had been set up. And if they knew that much, that meant they had a snitch, a statement, a witness, and now they would have the dope, too.

"I knew that I should have killed that ho!" Blue shouted.

"What are you talking about?" Bacon asked.

"I'm talking about your bitch, nigga."

"Who, Red?"

Blue huffed and shook his head. "That bitch is scandalous."

"How you figure Red had something to do with this?"

"Man, open your damn eyes!" Blue shouted. "How many people knew we was going to New York tonight? Now, how many of them ain't here?"

The feds piled Bacon and Blue into the U-Haul and drove them back to where Corey and Cavi had been stopped. The agents pulled them out of the truck and stood them at the back of the U-haul so they could watch more agents disassemble the sidewalls of the carrier truck.

The power screwdrivers made short work of the hidden panels, and the agents pulled the fake metal sidewalls out of the truck. Stacks and stacks of kilos of cocaine were now visible.

"Whoa, it's snowing!" the agent shouted.

The agents broke into laughter, and began exchanging high fives. It was a great bust.

"Well, do you have anything to say for yourself?" the agent asked Bacon.

Bacon shook his head and looked off into the distance. He didn't want to go to jail for a bullshit weed case tonight, but now it appeared that he was going to go to jail for much more. He had just beat one case; now he had an even bigger one. And they had him cold on this one. There would be no beating this case.

"I'm going to have to thank my friend Detective Thomas of

the Detroit Police Department for such a wonderful tip!" the agent declared.

A tear started to form in the corner of Bacon's eye. He was about to leave Red out on the streets alone once again. Would she stay faithful this time? Would the letters and visits come? He hoped in his heart that things were different this time, and that Red would really stay down for him. She had changed, and he had opened up his heart to her. He really loved her as wifey.

Bacon felt a sadness so profound that it touched every corner of his soul. The tear that was welling in the corner of his eye rolled down his cheek. He knew that he was about to go away for a long long time.

$\mathcal{W}$ ho is it?" Terry shouted, as she walked to the front door.

"Special Agent Rhonda Davenport."

"Who?" Terry asked. She opened the front door to find a strange woman and two police officers standing before her.

"Rhonda Davenport, Special Enforcement Agent, Child Protective Services," Rhonda said, holding up her badge and ID. "Are you Terry Washington?"

Terry nodded. "I am."

"Is Mr. Mekel Chambers home also?"

"He is, you want to speak to him?"

"Is the child, Mekel Chambers Jr., also on the premises?"

"What's this about?" Terry asked, growing suspicious.

Agent Davenport handed Terry some folded papers. "This is a court order, awarding custody of the child known as Mekel Chambers Jr. to the state. I have been ordered to enter the premises and take guardianship of the child, who hereafter shall be a ward of the State of Michigan."

"What? What are you saying?"

"Where is the child, ma'am?"

"Mekel!" Terry screamed.

Agent Davenport and the two officers tried to push past Terry and walk into the house. Terry held the door and blocked their entrance.

"Mekel!"

Mekel raced down the stairs. "What the fuck is going on?"

"Ma'am, you have to step aside!" one of the officers commanded.

"What? You can't just come in my house!" Mekel shouted.

"They have a warrant!" Terry shouted hysterically. "They are trying to take MJ."

"What? Are you crazy? You can't take my son!"

"Sir, we have a court order!" Davenport told him.

"I don't give a fuck what you have!" Mekel shouted. "You ain't taking my son!"

"Sir, step aside, or you will be arrested for civil disobedience and unlawful conduct, as well as interfering with an officer discharging a lawful order of the state."

"You are not taking my son!" Mekel repeated.

"Noooooo!" Terry screamed. The other children heard the commotion and gathered in the kitchen, cold with fear.

Davenport stepped to the side, and one of the officers grabbed Terry. Mekel tried to pull him off of her, but was grabbed by the other officer. He broke away, and shoved the officer down.

"Sir, you will be charged with assault on a police officer!" Davenport shouted. "You're just making things worse for yourself."

The second officer pulled out his nightstick. Mekel ran toward him and tackled him. The first officer got up and raced to help his fellow cop. Davenport went for the door, but Terry barreled toward her.

"Bitch, you not taking my son!" Terry shouted.

The first officer pulled out a small can of mace and sprayed Mekel in his eyes. Mekel began swinging wildly; then the second officer struck him in his stomach with his nightstick, sending him sprawling to the ground.

The first officer pulled Terry off of Agent Davenport and slammed her against the wall. Davenport helped restrain Terry while the officer cuffed her. At the same time the second officer hooked up Mekel.

"What the fuck is going on?" Mekel shouted, eyes streaming from the pepper spray.

"Sir, we have a court order to take custody of Mekel Chambers Jr.," Davenport explained.

"Why?" Terry demanded. "What did we do?"

"I really can't discuss the case . . ."

"You're the caseworker, ain't you?" Terry asked.

"Well . . . yes."

"Then tell us what the fuck is going on!"

"We've had some very serious allegations made against you."

"What kind of allegations?" Mekel asked.

"Allegations of child abuse of a physical and sexual nature," Davenport explained.

"What the fuck are you talking about?" Mekel shouted. "That's my son!"

"And you've shown a lot of restraint here today," the first officer said sarcastically. "You got a temper, buddy."

"I would never do anything to hurt my son!" Mekel said.

"This is just the beginning of the investigation," Davenport explained. "Granted, this definitely doesn't look good on your part. You've shown a propensity for violence and a lack of rationality in all of your actions today."

"What kind of investigation?" Terry wanted to know.

"Look, we're going to take custody of all of your children

until the investigation is complete," Davenport explained. "Child Protective Services will investigate the allegations, and report back to the court. If the court decides that the allegations are without merit, custody of the children will be returned to you."

"Where are they going?" Terry cried.

"That's for the courts to decide," Davenport told them.

"Allegations?" Mekel shouted. "What fucking allegations? From who? We don't go anywhere, and we don't fuck with anybody!"

"Who could have done this?" Terry cried out. "Who lied on us?"

"I can't give you any names," Davenport told them.

"We don't fuck with nobody!" Mekel repeated. "My son don't have a bruise on him!"

"We're going to investigate the claims," Davenport told him. "We have to. For the safety of the child."

"Put yourself in my shoes," Terry cried. "Think about what you're saying. Think about what you're doing! If these were your children, and someone showed up one day out of the blue and said that they were taking them, how would *you* react?"

"Ma'am, we have reports that you abused the baby previously," Davenport told her. "You tried to kidnap the said victim and dropped him, resulting in damage."

Terry shook her head and burst into tears. "No! That was an accident! Mekel, tell her that was a mistake!"

"Who did this, lady?" Mekel shouted. "We have a right to know! If it were your child, you would want to know who lied on you!"

"We have a confidentiality clause that prevents me from revealing the person who reported the abuse," Davenport told him.

"You would want to know if it was you!" Terry shouted.

"I can't give you her name," Agent Davenport told them.

"Her?" Terry looked over at Mekel.

"It better not be!" Mekel said, knowing what Terry was thinking.

The two officers walked into the residence to retrieve Mekel Jr. and the other children.

"Was she a tall, slender, red-skinned bitch with long red hair?" Terry asked.

Agent Davenport looked startled.

"I'ma kill that bitch!" Mekel shouted.

"Young man, you are not making this any better," Davenport said sternly. "You don't want to be heard by the officers making a terroristic threat."

"I don't give a fuck! I'm going to kill that bitch!" Mekel cried out.

Terry's cries grew louder and the tears flowed faster. All of the work she had done with her psychiatrist over the last nine months was quickly coming undone. She was unraveling mentally. She could see herself stabbing Red with a pair of scissors. "I'm going to kill you, Red."

CHAPTER FORTY-FIVE

*A*re you Internal Affairs?" Red asked.

"I am," Detective Marquez Nuñez told her. "And who are you?"

"A friend."

"I don't know," Nuñez said, eyeballing her figure. "I would definitely remember a friend like you."

Red smiled. Marquez Nuñez was cute. He was well manicured, well groomed and well dressed. He cut a fine figure in the Brioni suit that he was wearing.

"And if I would have known there were detectives like you walking around, I would have committed a crime a long time ago," Red teased back.

"That's okay, we're here now." Nuñez smiled. "Can I pat search you?"

Red laughed. "I'm sure you would love to do that."

"So, what can I help you with, Miss . . ."

"Friend," Red told him. "For now, just call me a friend."

"What can I do for you, friend?"

"I need for you to make me a promise."

"I don't do promises," Nuñez told her. "Sorry."

"Oh, well, then can you get me an Internal Affairs detective who does?"

"Why do you need an IA detective?" Nuñez asked, lifting an eyebrow.

"I'll discuss that with someone who is willing to make me a promise and keep his word."

Detective Nuñez held up his hands. "Okay, you got me. Let's hear it."

"You don't make promises, remember?"

"Okay, I'm willing to bend my policy."

"Promise me that if I give you something, you won't open it until tomorrow?"

Nuñez smiled. "Why would I promise that? You could be giving me a bomb, or a suicide note, or a letter telling me that you're going to kill someone. If I had evidence like that in my possession and didn't act on it . . ."

"I'm not giving you a bomb," Red promised.

"You won't even tell me your name."

"You'll have it in due time."

"What do you want to give me?" Nuñez asked.

"A package. It has a video, a statement, some DNA evidence, stuff like that."

"Does it involve a murder?"

Red shook her head. "No."

"You're giving it to an IA detective, so obviously it involves a police officer," Nuñez surmised. "Is anyone in immediate danger?"

"No."

"Why don't you want me to open it until tomorrow?"

"Do you agree to my terms?"

"What if I promise you, and then open it today anyway?"

"Then you lose my cooperation."

Marquez Nuñez extended his hand. "Give me your package."

"Tomorrow," Red told him.

"Tomorrow," Nuñez promised. "And if I do as you ask, I want your full cooperation in the matter. You come clean on everything, is that clear?"

Red nodded. "You got it."

Nuñez took the package from Red's hand and disappeared down the corridor.

Red turned and headed for the third floor of the police department.

Getting off the elevator, she ran into Detective Thomas.

"What are you doing here, Raven?"

"I need you," Red told him. "You said that if I needed you, you would be there for me."

"I am here for you."

"I have something that I want to give you."

"What is it?"

Red pulled a disc from her bag and handed it to Thomas.

"What is this, Raven?"

"It's evidence."

"Evidence?" Thomas lifted an eyebrow. "Evidence of what?"

"Of a serious crime that was committed."

"By who? By you?"

Red shook her head. "By a drug dealer named Catfish. He killed a friend of mine, and threatened to kill me. I have it all recorded. This is a copy of that recording."

"What are you into?" Thomas asked angrily. "Where did you get this?"

"I recorded it. I knew that he did it, and I wanted to get evidence of it, so I recorded him."

"And where is this gentleman right now?"

"He's locked up on other charges. He's a very powerful man. He arranged it all from prison."

"And how do you know this person?"

"My best friend used to date him. She would testify against him as well, but he had her killed."

Thomas shook his head. "Raven, you're into too much shit."

"I'm coming clean and turning over a new leaf. Isn't that what you wanted?"

"Yeah, but damn!"

"Well, don't ask me to come clean if you can't deal with it."

"I can deal with it," Thomas told her. "What else is there? What else are you hiding?"

"Nothing!"

"Ezekiel, Raven. Tell me about Ezekiel!"

"I don't know about Ezekiel! Q killed him!"

"Why do you say that? What do you know?"

"I know that Q admitted to killing him."

"That's two murders, Raven. Two that you are intimately involved in. I can't protect you if you're not honest with me!"

"I am being honest. That's all I know. I've given you what I know. This man Catfish killed my friend and Q killed his friend. Now I'm stuck picking up the pieces of my life."

"So what am I supposed to do with this?"

"You're a homicide detective! Listen to it, and investigate. She didn't deserve to die like that."

"Okay, I'll look into it."

"He needs to pay for what he did to her."

"You say that he's threatened to kill you?"

Red nodded.

Detective Thomas sighed. "Come and stay with me, where you'll be safe."

"I'm safe now."

"He's already killed one person from prison; doing you is nothing but a thing."

"Listen to the recording. He won't kill me. At least not yet. Not until he realizes that I recorded him and gave the tape to you."

"I'll safeguard this. He won't know we're on to him until after the grand jury has indicted his ass."

"Good." Red turned to leave.

"Where are you going?"

"I have to go see a friend."

"Be careful, Raven."

"Always."

CHAPTER FORTY-SIX

*C*atfish spied Red as soon as he walked into the visitation room. Her red hair, expensive clothing and sophisticated looks set her apart from the other visitors. She looked more like an attorney than a visitor. He would have loved the opportunity to pull Red into one of the restrooms and fuck the shit out of her, he thought.

Catfish approached the table and Red stood.

"Have a seat," she told him.

"I thought it was the man who stood up when the woman approached the table?" Catfish said jokingly.

"I guess whichever person is the bitch at the moment."

"What?"

"Sit down," Red demanded.

"This meeting is already getting off to a foul start." Catfish frowned. "Besides, didn't I tell your ho ass to let me know the next time you decide to pay me a visit?"

"This is strictly business."

"I sent you the manuscript," Catfish told her.

Red nodded. "I checked my PO box before I came."

Catfish smiled. "That shit is the bomb."

"I hope it is."

"Why don't you sit down?" Catfish asked.

"Why don't you?"

"Look, them guards is going to come over here and fuck with us if we just standing here."

Red seated herself. Catfish did the same.

"I wasn't planning on staying long." Red exhaled.

"Why'd you come in the first place?"

"I just wanted to make sure that the book was legit, and to update you on everything."

Catfish nodded. "Bitch, the book is legit. My nigga knocked that muthafucka out with lightning speed, and I read each chapter as he finished it. You think that first joint was the shit? This book is going to blow that one out of the water."

"And that's the whole book that you sent?" Red asked.

"Yeah? Damn, did you eat a bowl of retarded cereal this morning? How many times I gotta repeat myself?"

Red nodded and smiled. "I ate a plate of catfish."

"Did you eat the catfish's dick, too?"

"I ate the whole thing." Red smiled. "I fucked over that catfish real good."

Catfish leaned back in his chair and narrowed his eyes at her. "You better be careful when you try to fuck over a catfish. You know catfish sting."

"Not if you catch that muthafucka just right." Red smiled. "You see, the thing about a scavenger like that is that it's greedy. It'll eat anything you throw at it and that's what makes it so easy to catch."

"I see a bitch need her neck snapped this morning."

"I don't think so. Turn around."

Catfish turned and eyeballed the guard's station. Four guards were standing there watching him. "What the fuck is that?"

"I told the guard that I was going to give you some fucked-up news, and that they might need some extra security. So if you so much as blink wrong, they're going to have your ass on the floor, stomping you down like a cockroach."

"I can reach out and touch you, Red," Catfish said angrily. "Have you forgotten that? Ask your girl Sasha. Oh, that's right, you can't. She's dead."

Red smiled and shrugged. "You run your mouth too much. You talk like a bitch. No wonder you was the star in *Bitch Nigga, Snitch Nigga*."

"I'll slap the shit out of you and don't give a fuck about what them guards do."

"Do it!" Red challenged him. "You bad. Make your move."

"What are you here for today?"

"To let you know how you fucked yourself."

"I ain't worried about that little fifty thousand dollars, Red. You know what, you can keep that. I'ma put a fifty-thousand-dollar hit out on your head. So, that's a hundred grand that I'm out of. Deal with that, bitch."

Red laughed. "You're out of more than a hundred grand. You're out of time, you son of a bitch."

"How do you figure that?" Catfish waved his arms around the room. "All I got is time."

"Homicide is coming for your ass."

"Homicide already got me."

Red shook her head. "They are going to execute your ass for killing Sasha, and since you had it done from behind bars, the feds want to see you for running a continuing criminal enterprise from in prison. Since prison ain't stopping you from hurting society, they're going to want to transfer you to a maximum security federal prison out in Colorado. That way, you'll only get out of your cell an hour a day for recreation, and you'll have no contact with anybody in the outside world."

Catfish smiled. "Sounds like you got it all worked out."

"Yup, I have friends in high places," Red told him.

"Did your friends tell you about a little thing called evidence?"

Red reached into her pocket and pulled out a small digital recorder. She pushed playback.

"Did your friends tell you about a little thing called evidence?" the recorder repeated.

"Like I said, you talk like a bitch," Red told him.

Catfish's eyes bugged out of his head.

"Yeah, I recorded you the last time I was here, too. They have you on tape threatening to kill me, and bragging about killing Sasha."

"What the fuck did you do that for?" Catfish asked.

"Because you wanted to kill me. Having your ass on lockdown in Colorado 24-7 was the best way to save my own ass."

"And you think that you are going to be safe now?"

"They'll be putting you on lockdown soon."

"You're dead, Red."

"I'm leaving town, Catfish. I'm going to go and say good-bye to my stepfather and spend the night with him, and then no one in Michigan will ever see me again." Red stood.

"You're dead, your stepfather is dead, everyone you fuckin' associate with is dead. You can't run and hide anywhere. I'll find you if it takes every penny I have."

"Leave my stepfather out of this," Red told him.

"He's dead!"

"Good luck, Scavenger." Red walked away from the table. She knew that Catfish was fuming. Now, she just had to disappear and let her plan work. She knew that the first place Catfish was going to send his henchmen was to her mother and stepfather's house. *May they rest in peace.*

CHAPTER FORTY-SEVEN

*R*ed stood outside the hospital waiting for her attorney. She had hired one of Ohio's best real estate attorneys to represent her in the closing on Bacon's house. Red was determined that nothing go wrong this time. She needed the money to pay for her new house in Scottsdale.

Joel Weinstein pulled up in his black Lexus LS 460 and illegally parked. He climbed out and rushed up to the front entrance of the hospital.

"Hi, Raven," Weinstein said, hugging Red. "How are you, young lady?"

"I'm fine." Red smiled.

Weinstein looked around, taking in his environment. "Are you okay?"

"Yes, why?"

"Why'd you want to meet at the hospital?"

"Oh, because I needed to come here and visit a friend," Red explained. "I figured I may as well kill two birds with one stone."

"Oh, I was worried that you may have gotten sick or something."

Red shook her head. "I'm better than ever."

"That's a relief," Weinstein told her. "Well, we got really lucky that the couple didn't change their minds about the place."

"I know."

"They were really patient about the entire thing."

"I'll have to send them a nice card or something."

"That would be nice, I'm sure they would appreciate that," Weinstein told her. He reached into his briefcase. "Well, here is your check."

"Let's hope that I can cash it this time." Red laughed.

"No, this time it's good. All of the closing documents were in order, I made sure of it myself. Your check is as good as gold."

"Whew, that's a relief to hear," Red said, exhaling. "The Realtor in Scottsdale will be happy."

"What are you going to do with Gomez Realty?"

Red shrugged.

"Gloria and I were friends for a long time," Weinstein told her. He sighed. "I drive by that place and I can't believe that Schottenstein Realty is no longer. She thought of you like a daughter."

Red nodded. "I miss her."

"Honor her by continuing her legacy. Honor her by continuing to be successful."

"I will." Red leaned forward and gave him a hug. "Thank you, Joel."

"You're welcome, young lady. Well, I've got to go, I'm double-parked."

Red waved, turned and walked into the hospital, where she rode the elevator up to the third floor. She entered Q's room and found him watching television.

"What the hell are you doing here, Red?" Q asked angrily.

"I'm here to see you."

"Well, I don't want to see you!"

"Q, don't say that."

"Red, are you fucking crazy?"

"Q . . ."

"You shot me!"

"I was scared! Q, Bacon had kidnapped me, he was going to kill me!"

"Bullshit, Red! You could have shot that nigga! But you made your choice, so now stick with it."

"I'm not here to beg you to take me back, Q."

"Then what are you here for?"

"To say good-bye."

"Good-bye, Red," he said nastily.

"I want you to know that I really loved you. I still love you. Out of all the men in my life, I can really say that I loved you."

Q waved his hand around the hospital room. "And this is the way you show it?"

"I regret the way things turned out."

"I don't."

"But I don't regret ever loving you and having you in my life."

"I wish that I could say the same."

"Q, you can't say that you never loved me."

"Why can't I?"

"Because I'm not in jail."

"I'm not a snitch."

"You didn't tell the police, because you love me."

"I didn't tell the police because I'm going to kill you and your little boyfriend myself when I get out of here."

Q's words struck her to her core. "Don't say that, Q. Please don't say that you want me dead. You're the only one I ever felt really loved me."

"If you felt like that, then why did you shoot me, Red? Why?"

"I wasn't aiming for you. I was trying to shoot his ass!"

Q shook his head. "I don't believe that shit."

Red exhaled. "Well, it's the truth. Even if you don't believe me, Q, at least find it in your heart to forgive me."

"You're asking a lot, Red."

"I know. But trust me, Q. You mean so much to me."

Q shook his head and looked out the window.

"I'm leaving, Q. And I won't be back."

"Good luck to you and that bum."

"I'm leaving alone. I'm starting my life over again."

"Well, best of luck to you, Red. You don't have to worry about me snitching. And if I ever find it in my heart to forgive you, then I won't come after you. If I don't forgive you, I'm going to hunt you down, Red."

"Good luck, Q." Red tried to lean forward and kiss him. He lifted his hand, stopping her.

"Just go, Red."

Red walked out of the room, and walked out of the hospital and climbed into Bacon's blue Bentley Continental GT convertible. She was taking the car with her to Arizona. Scottsdale, Arizona, to be exact. There, she was going to reopen Gomez Realty, and sell multimillion-dollar desert real estate to wealthy golfers and retirees. She was going to start her life anew in a desert paradise. Her only regret was that Q wouldn't be coming with her.

Red cranked up the Bentley and headed for the highway. Arizona was a long drive away.

CHAPTER FORTY-EIGHT

*T*he doorbell rang and instantly Jerome began cursing.

"Goddamn people disturbing my fucking dinner!" he shouted, pushing away from the table. "A man can't even have a peaceful dinner. If it ain't the damn telemarketers calling, it's somebody selling something at the damn door!"

Jerome stormed to the door and threw it open.

"What the fuck do you want?" he shouted.

"Are you Red's dad?" Poocus asked.

"No, I'm her stepfather!" Jerome told him. "What's the little slut done now?"

"She got you killed," Black told him, standing behind Poocus.

Poocus pulled a sawed-off shotgun from beneath his oversize shirt and aimed it at Jerome's stomach. Jerome tried to run, but Poocus pulled the trigger and blasted him off his feet.

Struggling to say something, Jerome lay on the ground, holding his stomach, his intestines spilling out. He knew that his time had come. He knew that these goons were not going to let him live. He just thanked God that his wife worked at night and that she wasn't home right now. Despite all his faults, all his actions, all his proclamations, he truly loved her.

Poocus stepped inside, stood over Jerome and squeezed the trigger once again.

"Check the rest of the house!" Black ordered. He and Poocus raced through the apartment, searching to see if anyone else was home. Black looked beneath the master bed, while Poocus checked the closet. Black searched the pantry; Poocus turned his attention toward the bathroom. They found no one.

"C'mon, let's get out of here," Poocus said.

He and Black retreated to the street and climbed into their hooptie and drove away.

CHAPTER FORTY-NINE

*D*etective Thomas strolled into the police department and quickly found himself cornered by three plainclothes detectives.

"Detective Thomas?" one of the men inquired.

"Yeah?" Thomas answered suspiciously.

"Your weapon please, Detective," another gentleman asked.

"What's going on here?" Thomas demanded. "What's the meaning of this?"

Another officer patted him down, looking for his gun.

"Hey, get your fucking hands off of me!" Thomas said, pushing the man away.

Two of the men grabbed Thomas and slammed him against a nearby wall.

"We can do this the polite way, or the rough way," one of the men told him. "I'm Detective Robinson, this is Detective Johnson, that's Detective Lynn, we're IAD."

"Okay, but what the fuck is going on here?" Thomas asked.

Detective Marquez Nuñez strolled from around the corner. "What's going on is that I finally got your ass."

"Man, get a fucking hobby!" Thomas demanded.

"I got a hobby, and a job, too." Nuñez smiled. "It's busting crooked cops like you."

"You've gone too far now," Thomas told him. "The lieutenant is going to have your shield!"

"I doubt that," Nuñez said. "The lieutenant ain't touching this one with a ten-foot pole."

"When he finds out that you've taken my gun . . ."

"And your shield," Nuñez said, unclipping Thomas's badge from his waist.

"You don't have the authority to do that!" Thomas shouted. "You can't put me on administrative leave!"

"Admin leave?" Nuñez threw his head back in laughter. "You wish you were going on leave. You're going to prison, buddy."

"What the fuck are you talking about?" Thomas asked.

"Detective Thomas, you're under arrest for rape," Detective Nuñez told him.

"Rape? What the fuck are you talking about? Have you lost your mind?"

"No, but you must have."

"Rape? Rape who? When? Where?"

"Does the name Raven Gomez sound familiar?"

"Raven Gomez!" Thomas exclaimed. "I didn't rape no Raven Gomez!"

"Do you deny knowing her?" Detective Lynn asked.

"No, I know her," Thomas told them.

"How do you know her?" Detective Johnson questioned.

"I was investigating a case."

"The Ezekiel Morrison case," Nuñez confirmed.

"Yeah, that's right."

"She was a suspect?" Detective Johnson asked.

"Think carefully before you answer that question, Detective," Robinson told him.

Thomas shrugged. "You could say that."

"That's all I needed to hear," Nuñez said.

"What are you talking about?" Thomas demanded.

"I have a sworn affidavit from Ms. Gomez stating that you raped her," Nuñez explained. "You forced her to have sex with you in exchange for dropping her as a suspect in the Ezekiel Morrison case."

"That's ridiculous!" Thomas shouted, his face turning red with anger.

"You deny having sex with her?" Detective Lynn asked.

"This is bullshit!" Thomas told him.

"Did you have sex with her?" Detective Robinson repeated.

"I want a lawyer," Thomas said.

"Wise choice." Detective Lynn smirked.

"Your lawyer ain't gonna be able to help you out of this one," Nuñez leaned in and told Thomas. "I got DNA evidence, I have you on video having sex with her and I have her statement. Your ass is through."

"Having sex with a material witness?" Detective Johnson shook his head. He grabbed Thomas's hands and handcuffed his wrist. "Your goose is cooked."

"You Internal Affairs muthafuckas are some real pieces of shit!" Thomas said.

"We don't rape witnesses," Detective Lynn commented.

"I told your ass that I was going to get you." Nuñez smiled. "I knew that your punk ass was dirty."

Detective Thomas lunged at Nuñez, and the others grabbed him.

"I saw Ms. Gomez," Nuñez told him. "She's fine as hell. I wouldn't mind hitting that pussy. But rape? Giving up my career for it? You're more desperate and pathetic than I thought."

"Fuck you!" Thomas spat.

"No, you just fucked yourself, Detective," Nuñez replied.

"Actually, I think Ms. Gomez fucked him," Detective Lynn said, laughing. "You thought you had some free pussy, and she set your stupid ass up."

Detective Thomas shook his head and looked down. She had set him up. She had used him to do her dirty work. He had gotten rid of everyone who had done her dirty, then she threw him to the wolves. She truly was a dirty bitch.

CHAPTER FIFTY

*S*aguaro Estates was one of Scottsdale's premier communities. It sat among the gentle rolling hills of the desert, surrounded by luxury golf resorts and decadent shopping malls. It was a community for Scottsdale's rich and famous.

Red's new mansion was a $2 million, 7,000-square-foot, adobe-style hacienda, nestled on two acres of landscaped desert. The home boasted six bedrooms, five and a half baths, a five-car garage, a home theater, a formal and informal dining area, two living areas, a game room, a hot tub with luxury pool and vanishing edges and separate *casita*. Imported Italian marble floors ran throughout the home, while European granite kitchen countertops, a luxurious master bath containing a sauna and a barrel tile roof finished up the home's luxury.

Red strolled across the marble floor of her family room and headed outdoors to her swimming area. She unwrapped the towel around her waist and slid into her steaming hot tub and relaxed.

A bowl of fruit sat next to the hot tub, as well as a bottle of Cristal. Red lifted the bottle and poured herself a full crystal flute of the golden, bubbly champagne. She was already enjoying her new life in Scottsdale. The malls were like nothing she had seen before. Most of them were high end, brimming with luxury shops. It was going to take her a year to hit all of the shops and the malls in Scottsdale. She had already hit up one and had been hit on by two Black physicians during the course of her brief shopping excursion. Rich men were falling out of the sky.

Red sipped at her champagne and thought about her life, about what had happened to her. She didn't want to think about her mother, and whether or not Catfish had sent his boys to her house yet. She had hardened her heart and accepted the fact that her mother wasn't going to be in her life anymore, so she might as well take a chance on hitmen getting her in order for them to get that bastard Jerome. Deep down, Red hoped that they would strike at night, when her mother was at work and Jerome was there by himself. That would be the best scenario. Briefly she thought about one day driving to Las Vegas, grabbing a burn-out cell phone and calling. Hopefully her mother would answer and tell her that Jerome was dead, but that was in the future. Right now, she just wanted to relax and get settled.

Red also thought about Detective Thomas. She had enjoyed his company when he was around. *I wouldn't have fucked with him if he didn't keep questioning me about Ezekiel,* she convinced herself. *He was a good man.*

By now, Internal Affairs would have made their move on him. She had set him up perfectly by recording their lovemaking, and screwing raw dog. He would have a hard time explaining why she had his DNA inside her and the report from the doctors from the hospital definitely sealed the case. She could just see his face when he read it. Red threw her head back in laughter. Bruised pelvic area, rough abrasion signaling forced entrance.

Too bad you had a big dick, she thought. *It was good but they're not always a good thing to have, especially when a bitch is accusing you of rape.* Red laughed again.

And then there was Bacon and Blue. Two assholes for the price of one. She could just see the look on Bacon's face when the police searched the dope truck. *He probably shitted himself. Yeah, he had better get himself a prison girlfriend this time, because there will be no coming out of this one. This time, he was caught red-handed. He and Blue should try to be cellmates; maybe they could fuck each other.* She emitted another wicked laugh.

And then there was Terry and Kera. Kera was going to be going away for a long time. She had set her up cold. *The stupid, greedy bitch,* Red thought. *She couldn't just leave well enough alone. Acting all religious and high and mighty, and then stealing seven days a week. Hopefully they'll put her in a cell full of big-ass dykes.* And she could just see Terry's face when Child Protective Services showed up at her door. *That bitch is probably in shock therapy by now.*

Red took another sip of her champagne and laughed again. She still had the recording of Terry admitting to shooting up her house and trying to kill Kera. She would wait a couple of months, and then send that recording to the police as well. That way, just when that bitch thought her troubles were over, she would get hit with the biggie. Mekel would probably leave that bitch just to keep from paying any more of her legal fees! Red broke into laughter at the thought of it.

She had taken care of all of her enemies. She had been living high on the hog in Scottsdale for a few weeks, and she didn't have a care in the world. If only she had Q here with her in the hot tub. Being free and clear and getting away from Detroit with her own money had always been her dream. But she always thought that she would be doing it with Q.

A hot wind blew across the desert, and Red looked up into the star-studded sky. The desert wind reminded her of Mexico, and she made a silent promise to herself to return there. She loved Mexico now. Being there with Q had really been fun; even though Bacon had spoiled her the last time she was there, it had been more exciting with Q. Maybe one day, he would forgive her.

Chass Reed was that bitch's name, Red recalled. She was all over Q, and Q was acting like that bitch was something special. She would have to get rid of old Chass in order for Q to see clearly. Red was the only woman for Q, and Q was the only man for her. He just needed to be reminded of that. Sometimes an extra bitch in the picture complicated things. *A nigga can't see straight until he's fucked her and got it over with. Then he realizes where he belongs and takes the dick back home. That's all Q needs. To just hit Ms. Chass and get it over with.* She would check on him in a few months and see where things were at.

A ringing tone broke Red from her thoughts.

"What the fuck?" Red eyeballed her cordless phone. She had just had her telephone cut on and it was a new number. *Who in the fuck could be calling?* she wondered.

The phone rang again.

Red pushed the "talk" button on the phone. "Hello?"

"Hey, Red."

"Who the fuck is this?"

"Who the fuck you think this is?"

The voice sounded eerily familiar. "Catfish?"

"That's right, bitch! I told you, you can run, but you can't hide."

"How the fuck are you calling me?" Red panicked. "How did you get this number?" She was too dumbfounded to offer a different response.

"Somebody should have told you, Red. The thing about legit

money is that it's easy to track. Somebody also should have told you I bury bodies in the desert."

Red hung up her telephone, jumped out of the hot tub, ran into her house and locked the door. Her breath had rushed out of her body, and her heart beat like an African drum. She nervously scanned around the interior of her mansion, afraid to move, afraid to go upstairs, afraid to grab her keys and run for the garage. She hadn't taken the time to go and buy a gun yet, because she hadn't been in a rush to do so.

Red's heart did a somersault in her chest, as her doorbell chimed.

It chimed again.

A voice rang out from the other side of her door. "You can run but you can't hide!"

Red fell to the floor in tears.

Catfish had found her.

Acknowledgments

My sons and legacy: Valen Mychal, what can I say, you keep me proudly smiling. Victor Amon, what can I say, you keep me believing.

My best girlfriends: Mary Lilley and Valerie Hunter, love you guys!

The team at Atria Books: Judith Curr, Malaika Adero, Nancy Inglis, Todd Hunter, thank you for the fifth time!

My loving and drama-filled family: The Stringers in the house!

Distributors, bookstores, media, fans and readers: Without you, there is no me and TCP.

To my homies on lock with love: Chancey (West Coast) Fuller, Lloyd Black, Rodney R. Stringer, Rodney E. Stringer, Rudolph Lynch, be easy and rest up.

To my legal eagles: Michael Anthony Law & Staff, F. Robert Stein, thank you for keeping the hounds at bay.

To my financial support: Arnell Hurt, the world's kindest accountant and friend.

To my authors, thank you for writing incredible stories.

Last, but never least: My TCP staff that labor daily with me to get the damn thing's done! Matthew Roberson, Christina Carter, Valerie (leap graphics), Maxine Thompson, Lisa Woodward (welcome back), Sharon Ballew, Frankie Stringer (road dawgz).

My mothers: Eula Thompson and Elder Vera Jackson.

It's the G-O-D in me, Lord and Savior, thank you for your grace, mercy and favor.